ONE HAND TO HOLD, ONE HAND TO CARVE

by

M.Shaw

featuring illustrations by
Echo Echo

edited by Alex Woodroe

Content Warnings are available at the end of this volume.
Please consult this list for any particular subject matter
you may be sensitive to.

TENEBROUS

PRESS

One Hand to Hold, One Hand to Carve
© 2022 by M.Shaw and Tenebrous Press

Production of this novel was made possible in part by a grant from the Regional Arts & Culture Council. Visit https://racc.org/ for more information.

Published by Tenebrous Press.
Visit our website at www.tenebrouspress.com.

First Printing, April 2022.

ISBN: 978-1-7379823-5-7

Front cover illustration and interior illustrations by Echo Echo.

Cover design by Matt Blairstone.

Formatting by Lori Michelle.

Printed in the United States of America.

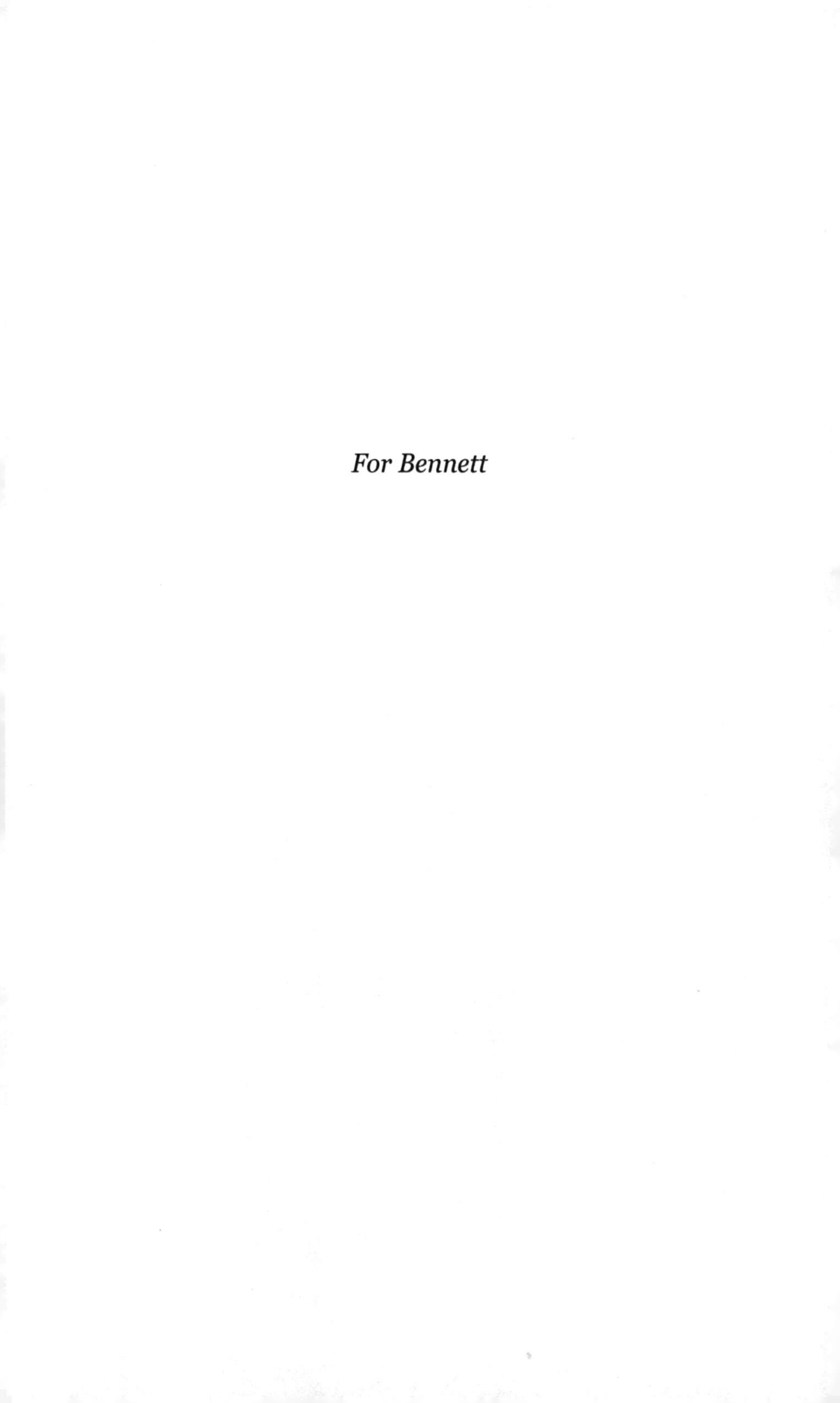

For Bennett

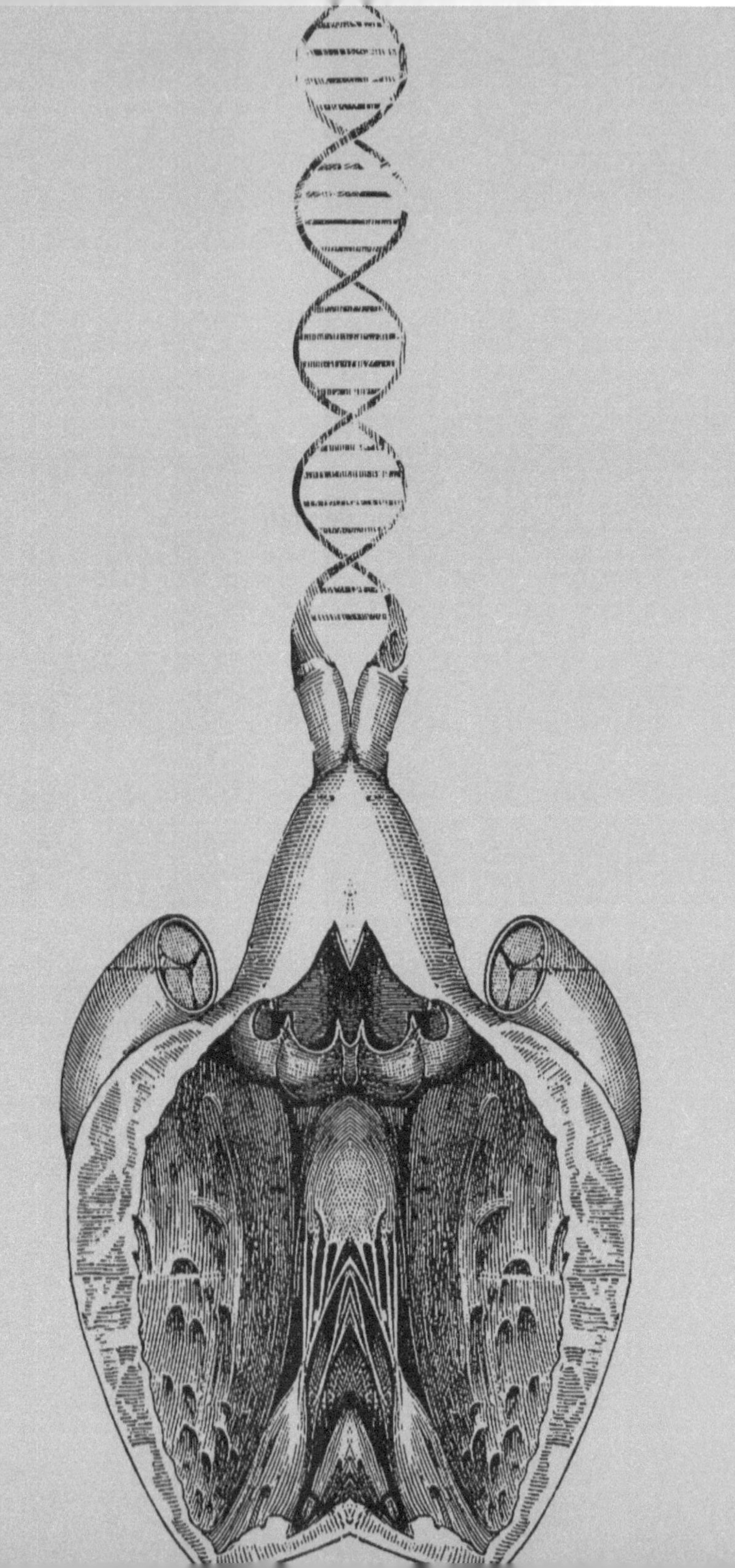

ALSO FROM TENEBROUS PRESS:

Green Inferno: The World Celebrates Your Demise
edited by Matt Blairstone

In Somnio: A Collection of Modern Gothic Horror
edited by Alex Woodroe

COMING SOON:

Lure
a novella by Tim McGregor

Crom Cruach
a novella by Valkyrie Loughcrewe

CHAPTER 1

THEY AWAKE ON the table, in the dark, breathing in the meaty scent of death soaked in formaldehyde. The unpleasant knowledge of this smell is their first thought. Their second thought is that it is the smell of their own bodies wafting out of their open cavities. What was, moments ago, a human cadaver bisected to display a cross-section, has become two men with half a body, lit suddenly by the heat of consciousness, newborn in their decrepitude. Their exposed cavities face each other, forming a V where they were cleaved apart, edges ragged with tissue that rumples like lace trim. Their exposed organs pulse gently with new life, close enough for each of them to feel the warmth radiating from the other.

What comes next is the burning sensation of air brushing against the raw wound that covers each man from crown to crotch. A body recovering from hypothermia will gradually come to understand how much pain it is in as it thaws, and there is no shock colder than death where the flesh is concerned. As the pain builds, they are aware of it mostly as a curiosity, another fact among many that they struggle to reconcile with the impossibility of their awakening.

Their bodies would form mirror images of one another, but for the asymmetry of the conventional human corpse. The biggest difference is that only one of them feels a heart beating behind his ribs. This one—the left side—runs his finger along the ridge of his cranium, careful not to touch the soft gray matter inside. He tries to vocalize, but the sounds he produces are malformed by his half-mouth, his half-tongue.

The other one can hear the sounds only distantly. His ear faces down at the table, away from his brother, but he recognizes the source immediately. This is his first deduction: that there must be another half of him, somewhere nearby. He pushes a response from his throat, clumsy as it is. "Ah woo a'hwake?"

His brother tries, again, to speak. "Yeh," he manages. "Uh I cuh . . . I cuh . . . I cah nah hfee woo."

What would be gibberish to any other ear is given meaning by their parallel experience. Who better to understand than the only other creature on Earth who can?

"I cah nah shee woo eefah. Buh I wuh wike if I cuh . . . if I could."

The man with the heart obliges, gripping the edge of the table to lever himself upright, twisting to drop his leg over the side. Formaldehyde pours from his cavity, cascading over bare organs, puddling beneath the edge of the table. His foot lands in the puddle when he hops down. He slips and nearly falls, catching himself with his elbow, then staggers more carefully and straightens on the leg.

His brother hears the sharp clang of the elbow on the stainless steel surface. "You ohay?"

"Yeh."

"Dih a'yfing faw ouch?"

The man with the heart pats the soft edges of his share of the organs. "Nuh. Nu'hing feh. Fell. Nu'hing fell." He pivots, bit by bit, hand on the table to steady himself, until he faces across it. And there, looking back at him, is his other half. This is the true moment of his birth, as it is anyone's: the first confirmation that he has not come into the world to find himself alone.

They see each other, now, in a reflection that no two

people have gazed upon before. Not a mirror image, or a photo, or a copy; each one looking at a body much like his own, and yet an entire separate person. Not a twin, but a kind of equal-opposite, naked and raw at the moment of their birth, with the dawning knowledge that the man across the table, looking back at him with a single eye, is having exactly the same thoughts. They are so transfixed that, for a brief moment, they cease to feel the burning of the air against their organs, or the terror of standing upright with their body cavities open. All each man has is the other, and maybe this is all each man needs, for now.

Eventually, the mere sight of each other is no longer answer enough for all their questions.

"Ah you wha' I wook wike?" says the heartless one, shame pushing his voice into a lower register.

They are two halves of what was once a middle-aged man, and not a conventionally attractive one by most measures. Their skin has drained of the color it once had, and their movements are stiff and slow, heavy with the ghost of rigor mortis.

"I'm sowwy," says the heart, even as he tries to find beauty in their sagging flesh, their wiry body hair, their toenails the color of pus. He wipes away a half-formed tear and, seeing no echo of this gesture in his brother, reflects that this is the first significant difference he has seen between them. He wonders if perhaps feelings are born in the heart after all. "You'a da white side."

"And you'a da weft."

And so they have put names to each other. The second connection of their relationship: first recognition, now identification. Right and Left.

So named, they converse, as much to compare thoughts as to practice articulating their consonants. They establish that neither of them remembers dying, or who they were before they died, or how it was that they came to live again. Neither of them remembers a family, a profession, a language other than English, a faith. Neither of them knows if their skin will heal over their open cavities, or if they will be like this forever. They know very little besides each other.

"I don't think we can stay here," says Right, when the conversation lulls. His eye sweeps over this workshop of the body, full of tables like the one they were on a minute ago. This is a school, he realizes, a school of anatomy. All the tables are empty, but the same embalmed odor pervades the entire facility. "This is a place for the dead, not the living."

"Living." Left hold his hand before his face.

"Like us," says Right. "We're alive, aren't we?"

"But where would we go?" asks Left, still staring at his hand. He is fascinated by the creases of his palm, the whorls of his fingerprints; terrified of what it means to live inside such complexity while simultaneously in awe of it. He wonders if it's correct to think that these fingerprints once belonged to a different person, and if so, whether anyone else has ever passed on their fingerprints to another like this.

Right considers the question. Where do I want to go, he asks himself, imagining rooms more pleasant than this one. Places with generous chairs and tables meant for dining, lights that are soft and warm, windows that show a world more beautiful than this human cutting room. "How about a cottage?"

"A cottage," Left says flatly.

Right nods, cautious not to do it too vigorously as he holds his posture. "You know, a little house in the woods, away from this. No stainless steel, no smell of decay. A place with a garden, maybe even some animals. A porch where we could sit and carve little figures out of wood. You could hold the block steady while I work with the knife."

"I meant, where can we go *now*," says Left. "I'm thinking more along the lines of one of those motels with weekly rates."

"Oh. Well. Yeah," says Right. "I guess that makes more sense in the short term. The cottage can come later. We'll just have to find one, and some woods."

"It does sound nice," says Left. "Maybe one day."

They experiment more with moving around. By themselves, they can only hop, which poses problems given the delicate, unsteady towers of their bodies. One hand is not enough to hold everything in place. Left's intestines fall out during one attempt, and it takes both of them working in concert to fit everything back where it belongs. Eventually, they realize that if they each wrap their arm around the other's hip, they can hug their bodies together and approximate a two-legged walk.

It is an awkward process, shuffling themselves together without being able to look where they are going. Right gropes for Left's hip once they are close enough, guiding them in. In the moment before their open sides meet, Left wonders if their half-brains will meld together when they touch. His heart quickens with the fear that these few minutes were all he had with his brother, before they are unified into a single body again.

Right, meanwhile, wonders if their organs will spill into each other's cavities while they are together. He imagines them mingling and sticking, rendering him unable to separate from his twin, and this fills him with an anxiety not quite parallel with Left's.

Left feels the hand on his hip, and reciprocates, and it is done. No fusion occurs. They still cannot see each other, but they can feel the soft wax and wane of each other's lungs, never quite in sync.

"I'll step first," says Right. "When you see my foot land, then you step."

It is not a perfect plan. Left's first step is more of a hop, causing them both great pain as the edges of their pelvic bones scrape together. They realize each one needs to lean slightly on the other as he steps. This works better, but creates a clownish, swaying gait, as they find when they discover a mirror in the nearby locker room. They also find a set of hospital scrubs and manage, while seated on the bench, to shuffle their bodies into the trousers, the shirt.

At a nurse's station, they find a pair of crutches. Left adopts one. Adding it to the rhythm of their motion, they practice until they are able to walk reliably, learning to sense each other's movements through touch. First the crutch and Right's foot, then Left's foot swinging between them. The sensation between them is friction on parts of the body that should never experience it, and they quickly find that pain has become a secondary language through which they communicate unspoken. They hobble down the hallways of the empty hospital wing, a work in progress, a labor of love.

They find the exit. It's dark outside, but not so dark as inside the building. Encased in a single garment, "walking" with the crutch, they appear to any incidental observers as a sickly, disoriented, injured man. As such, they are largely ignored by the few other people walking the streets this time of night, who do not want to be reminded of the frailty of their own bodies so explicitly.

The smells outside are mercifully fresher than those in the lab. The school is in a suburban area, where the air is thick with moisture and floral blooms. They meander barely-lit streets, crowded on either side by dense brush that blends together in the dark, forming an endless tangled, black mass. Air conditioners hum all around them in one collective harmony, like a call to prayer.

In the privacy of the side streets, they practice talking as if from a single mouth. They cannot read each other's thoughts, but with their single brain hemispheres so close, their newly awakened spinal nerves firing in tandem, it feels so much like they could, if only they tried hard enough. And so, they try words. Individual words, to start with. Left thinks of one, and focuses intently on sending it across the thin membrane of air where their minds intersect. Right listens for hints of the word, in whatever part of him is not a body part, and then they try to pronounce it together.

"Hwulghtwah," it comes out the first time.

"Fthelwroch," the second. Vowels and consonants

compound, forming a multi-tonal hiss that would normally be impossible for a mouth to produce.

Somehow, the longer they keep at it, the more they learn of each other's unspoken bodily code. By the time the sky grays with dawn's light, they are closer than ever. "Hwellyo," they drawl. Then, "Bwothwer. My bwot'ther." Then, "Hwoulfe. Hlove. Aye wlove yhoo." Left cracks a smile and the next word comes out unintelligible. If he knows nothing else, blanked as he is from the amnesia of death, he at least knows that he will always have this. He will always have another half who loves him.

They aren't able to find a motel before exhaustion overtakes them. Despite the rising sun, they find themselves quickly wearied from their first day of being alive, and bed down in a ditch alongside a cornfield. They cover themselves with brush and fall asleep, each one holding the other to himself, lest they lose track of each other while unconscious.

***

They do find a motel the following day, and struggle through explaining their needs to a concierge who stands as far back from the desk as he physically can while talking to them. He mutters something about payment and Right passes him a credit card they found in the road, covered with a patina of grime and nearly split down the middle. The concierge pushes a key across the counter and points them toward the rear of the building, clearly eager to end the encounter as quickly as possible and return to his phone game. If the card is declined when he tries to run it, the brothers never hear about it.

That night, they go around collecting change from beneath drive-thru windows, then stumble into a thrift store at dawn with enough for a cart full of 95-cent garments to share. Back at the motel, they find that their skin is indeed healing over their open sides. After a few days, when they are finally closed, and their faces have lost their grey-yellow pallor in favor of a more creamy pink, they begin to improvise a life.

After a few days of trial and error, they figure out how to rig, for each of them, a homemade prosthesis using pillows, broom handles, and duct tape, most of it pilfered from housekeeping. While wearing it, each brother is able to appear merely as a horribly disfigured man with half a face, rather than a reanimated corpse with half a body. A few more days experimenting with their accumulating piles of thrift clothes, and they develop their own preferences in outfits as well. Right finds that he favors whimsically patterned button-down shirts tucked into bluejeans; Left tries to follow suit, but eventually settles for his own, more casual outfits of track pants and oversized t-shirts.

On one of their thrift runs, they find an old laptop that still works within their budget. Right uses it to get a job when the motel starts being more aggressive about payment. It's just as well; their initially lean appetites are building by the day, and it's getting harder to feed themselves with scavenged coins. Left can't get a job; lacking a dominant hand, he cannot write and doesn't have the dexterity required for most types of work, so they both rely on Right's income. Left, instead, handles the domestic duties, buys groceries, cleans up, feeds them both. This is still difficult work, but in their motel room he is free to curse, stumble, and cry as much as he needs to push through it.

When they aren't busy trying to locate any bootstrap they can possibly pull, they discuss Right's idea of a cottage in more detail. Left suggests it should have two stories; Right adds that it should have a cellar. Right describes the stone hearth; Left, the split timber walls; Right makes sure to add a bench for them to work with wood; Left is not really interested in carving wood, but allows it. Day by day they map the interior, the décor, the garden, the surrounding woods. It becomes the source of joy they cling to, despite their frustrations, despite how little they are able to do together, much less by themselves.

At work, Right wears a headset through which he places

phone calls. After a time, when he has proven himself, he is moved to a desk where he receives calls instead. He follows scripts and enters commands into a computer. Easy work, as long as one can handle spending all day talking to people who are disgusted just to be having the conversation. No one except Left has ever reacted favorably to Right, so dealing with this is second nature. He takes the bus to work—almost 2 hours each way—until they come up with enough money to buy a used car, a badly rusted compact model that stops and goes and not much else.

Between calls, and during his breaks, he works on the cottage by himself, purely within his own imagination. At first, this only happens because Left doesn't want to talk about a workshop for wood carving, so it's the workshop he fleshes out first. After that, he finds that it keeps going. He adds a guest bedroom, and adorns the master with two twin beds, their headboards cut from the same giant tree trunk.

Soon, he realizes that there are now two versions of the cottage: the one that exists for both him and his brother, and the one that only exists for himself. He decides to hold on to the latter. It is just for him.

During the workday, Left also begins a project meant only for himself. He logs onto the internet and looks up methods of teaching himself to be ambidextrous. He finds videos, step-by-step guides, magazine articles, all of which he practices diligently. If only he could learn to articulate his hand the way Right can, he could provide for them in the same way his brother does.

His daily practice makes him more cognizant of his body, and this is how he notices what is happening to the edges of the bones close to his newly grown skin. Once smooth, where he and his brother were cut cleanly apart, he now finds them uneven. In some places, the bone strains against the skin. He begins feeling fatigued more easily, and wonders if this is why.

"Do you have a headache?" he asks Right after work one day.

"I . . . I do have a headache," says Right. "I've had one for days. How did you know?"

Left brushes the back of his hand across the edge of Right's cranium. Right feels the bumps now, vibrating gently against Left's carpals.

"What is that?" Right breathes. "Is that what's causing the pain? What's happening?"

"I think we're growing," says Left. "Or maybe more like expanding, or filling out. I've been getting tired more easily, too."

"So have I!" says Right. "It's why I've been drinking so much coffee, even though it mostly just gives me indigestion. Does it have to hurt so much?"

"Growing is hard work. That's what the internet says."

Right reaches his hand across his body and begins fondling the lumpy ridges of bone himself. There are times when he finds himself imagining the saw that must have cut them in half—a saw that is presumably still out there somewhere, tearing other bodies apart—and this is one of such times. He can almost picture it, as if in a memory: the long blade with a handle on either end, the kind of saw used to fell trees. The teeth that look like a hundred of the letter W with little spaces between.

"I'm honestly surprised you didn't notice it before," says Left.

"I noticed the pain," says Right. "But I didn't know what it was, so I just kept taking ibuprofen and trying to distract myself by thinking about something else."

"What could possibly distract you from this?"

Right doesn't want to say that he's spent the whole week busily working on his own version of the cottage. Today, it grew large enough that he had to move the guest bedroom upstairs to make room for the larger kitchen with the huge stone oven, where they'll bake their bread, kneading dough silently and perfectly in sync. One hand to press, one hand to fold. He considered how warm the upper floor would get in the summer, and noted to make sure the cottage has enough tall trees around to provide some relief. For reasons he can't quite name, he feels it would be a mistake to try to explain this to Left.

"A podcast I've been listening to," he says.

"What podcast?" says Left. "Can I listen?"

"I forget what it's called. I'll send you the link later. What do you think it means that we're filling out like this? That we'll become whole people?"

Left frowns. "We're whole people now."

"Okay, but you know what I mean," says Right. "Just, damn, imagine having two legs and being able to walk without a crutch. Let alone what you could do with two arms!"

Left flexes his fingers. In his research on ambidexterity, one thing he's done is look into the etymology of the word itself, "ambidextrous." It comes from combining the Latin words "ambi" (both sides) and "dexter" (right side). At first, learning this fact felt a bit like being written out of his own life, but once the initial feelings subsided, he began to find the idea strangely comforting. After all, "two left feet" is a metaphor for clumsiness. Why would "two right hands" be any different?

That's it: both of them are who they are. A Left cannot do the work of a Right, without becoming a Right himself. That's just the way it is. The natural thing is for them to work together, supporting each other, the way they always have and always will. And yet, here his brother is saying he wants them to break apart even further than they already have, eliminating the need for each other in their lives. Eliminating the entire purpose of their existence.

Right notices the downcast of his brother's eye. "What's the matter? Headache?"

"What if," says Left, "filling out doesn't make us more capable, just bigger? Then I'd be two Lefts, with two hands I can't use, and you'd be two Rights, with two capable hands and no heart."

As Left talks, Right imagines standing perpendicular to a full-length mirror, with his split side pressed to its surface, so that his body appears to duplicate itself in reverse. It sounds like a way to approximate what Left is describing. If only it were possible to also look at the mirror while standing next to it this way, he would at least be able to see what he would look like with an entire body. Having to content himself with fantasy, then, he imagines stepping away from the mirror and seeing the reflection step across the glass threshold to stand next to him. This way, they can look into the mirror together, and both see the whole picture.

Left continues, "All we could do then is take up more space. Our room would be more crowded, but with nothing to show for it. If that were the case, I'd prefer not to fill out. I'd want to stay the way I am."

"I don't know," says Right, still lost in his own fantasy. "I think I'd like to have it happen, regardless."

"I guess it's easy to feel that way, when you'd be the one with the good hands," says Left.

"I doubt it would happen that way," says Right. In his mind, the mirror-self he created turns to look at him, and he realizes that he has made not just a reflection, but an entire separate person. Not the same thing as what happened with him and his brother, when they were presumably cut apart by somebody else. This imaginary person would be, not a division, but a copy of himself just as he is. He wonders if a Reverse Right would be more agreeable about wanting to have a whole body, even without a heart.

"You're not going to leave me behind, are you?" says Left. "You're not going to get a second hand and decide you don't need me anymore, that you'd be better off by yourself while I bumble my way through life, helpless and alone?"

"What? No," says Right. "Why would I leave you?"

"Well, you do seem pretty excited about the idea of outgrowing me." Left's leg folds beneath him, and he crashes into the sofa.

Right crouches in front of him, bracing his palm on the floor for balance. "Growing doesn't necessarily mean outgrowing. Can't things be better for both of us?"

"But I'm your other half!" Left pleads.

Both of them have the feeling that this isn't exactly true, but neither can readily say why that is. Is it possible, they wonder, for something to be correct, even if it isn't the capital-T Truth?

"I'm not going to leave." It is hard to hug someone who has only one shoulder, especially when Right only has one shoulder himself. They manage it by draping their arms over each other's shoulders, then pressing their foreheads together, leaning into each other slightly so that their faces rest comfortably together.

"You promise?" says Left.

"If it makes you feel better, yeah."

Left sits up. "Well . . . all right. That'll have to do, I guess."

Left makes dinner. Early on, they tried chopping vegetables together, with Left holding the onion and Right chopping, but they quickly found it more efficient to simply buy vegetables pre-cut. Left misses those fumbling attempts, but dinner prep still calms his worry. It relaxes him, to work on tasks that are firmly within his abilities. He begins allowing himself to consider that the worst-case scenario may not be inevitable. Maybe he will grow a right hand that he can use. Maybe neither of them will grow another hand at all. And would that really be so bad, even if it means he can never hold and manipulate things like his brother can? If it means being by Right's side, maybe he would be willing to stay helpless forever.

***

Throughout the night, as he struggles to sleep, Right can't tear his thoughts away from the Reverse Right he created earlier. He sees Reverse Right hovering above his brother's motel bed. The longer Right lies awake, the more he modifies the visualization into someone more ideal. Someone he would want to look more like, if he could; someone smarter, who he could take advice from. He needs advice to untangle the confusion of his life, for the things he can't simply talk through with Left. Right wishes he could find such a person, or even be that person for himself, but this will have to be the best he can do.

First, he gives Reverse Right more hair, the way a younger-bodied man would have. Then more muscles, smoother skin, a more even beard, higher cheek bones, a broader shoulder. By the end, Reverse Right doesn't look all that much like him anymore. He looks like some other half-man, maybe a cousin or nephew to the balding, tired-looking, double-chinned man he sees in the mirror each day. Right finds himself envying this imaginary person, even though he only exists inside his own mind.

"I think I deserve a better name than Reverse Right," the man says.

"Okay," Right whispers.

Left does not wake.

"What name do you want?" Right asks. "Young Left? Strong Left?"

"No, those are just the same kind of thing," says Reverse Right. "I want a real name."

"Real?" Right repeats.

"Something like Ben, or Isaac, or Lincoln."

"I like Lincoln," says Right.

"Me too. That's who I'll be then."

"Can I be Lincoln too?"

Lincoln shakes his more chiseled half-head. "Only one of us can be Lincoln, otherwise there's no point. So it's me. My name. If we both had the same name, it would be like we're the same person."

"Aren't we part of each other?" says Right. "Like me and Left?"

"Good grief, no," says Lincoln. "I'm not part of anyone

but myself. Don't go dragging me into whatever weird logic you've got going on there. Look, if it helps then my last name can be Wright, with a W. So it still sounds like you want it to. Lincoln Wright."

Right sighs. He did not anticipate being this frustrated with his own imagination. "Well, nice to meet you Lincoln," he says. "I'm . . ." Left stirs in his sleep, a half-frown creasing his cheek, as if he were aware of the more ideal twin being imagined on top of him.

"What?" says Lincoln. "Are you ashamed of your name?"

"No," says Right. "I mean, yes. I mean, I guess it's not really a name, is it? Is Right a name?"

"Not the same way Lincoln is a name," says the imaginary twin. "It doesn't have anything to do with who you are, only how you relate to this other guy." He sweeps his hand over the sleeping Left. "I can see where you get your ideas about being part of somebody else."

"But I am part of him," says Right. "Literally. We were made from the same body."

"So are all full-blooded siblings," says Lincoln. "But once they separate themselves from their mother, then they're not the same anymore. Where you came from isn't a hundred percent of who you are, unless you choose to make it that way. Why should you be any different? You're your own person, now. You don't need him."

"What if I do? We need each other, my brother and I. You know who I don't need? You."

"Yeah, well, maybe I don't need you either," Lincoln growls. "I'm better than you in every way."

"You still don't have a heart," says Right.

"Oh, I do." Lincoln floats over and places his hand on Right's shoulder. "You just don't know it, because you can't imagine what it's like to have one. But that won't always be true, and someday you'll know I'm right."

"Right?" Left's voice rumbles softly, working its way out of sleep.

Lincoln is gone. Right realizes he was muttering to himself fairly loudly, narrating the entire conversation. "Sorry," he whispers.

"Are you hurt?"

"I had a nightmare."

"Oh," says Left. "Well, try to keep it down." Soon, he is asleep again.

Right spends the rest of the night with his face pressed into the pillow. Until the sun comes up, he can feel the imaginary brother's ghostly presence hovering over him, waiting for a chance to whisper in his ear. Finally, sunlight enters the motel room and Left awakens in earnest, and Lincoln is nowhere to be found.

Over breakfast, Left and Right compare notes on the ways they have grown during the night. Left has new bits of bone pressing against skin here and there. Right swears he can feel the beginning of an aorta. Left comments that Right looks tired.

"Growing is hard work," says Right. "Even in your sleep.

"Amen," says Left, rotating his plate so he can get at the food on the other side.

At work, seated at his desk, Right feels Lincoln appear behind him.

"Sorry if I was mean earlier," says Lincoln.

"Are you always like this?" says Right. "Maybe you can get away with being mean because you're better looking than I am. Maybe that's just who you are, and I'll have to let you be mean."

"Huh," says Lincoln. "And what about your personality is *just who you are*?"

"Not mean," says Right.

"Doesn't answer my question," says Lincoln.

"I'm busy now," says Right. "I'm at work. We'll talk later."

"I hope we will," says Lincoln. "I mean that."

Right snorts. "You do?"

"More than you know," says Lincoln. "Believe it or not, I

want to help you. Not my fault if you don't know your ass from a hole in the ground when it comes to certain things, but the reason I tell you the truth is because I genuinely care, and not just about myself."

"It sure doesn't seem like it," says Right, but Lincoln has already faded away to wherever it is he goes when they're not talking. Right tries to get himself back on task by working on his version of the cottage, although he's having a harder time picturing it than usual, today. When he tries to explore it, in his mind, it feels too big and too constricting at the same time. The version he's created is no longer comforting. And so, he grabs an imaginary sledgehammer and starts taking out walls. It's my cottage, after all, he thinks.

interlude

"Twin" means "to join together,"
and also "to make separate"

IN THOSE FIRST few weeks, when so many things seemed possible and so many others impossible, when the brothers had decided that Right should be the one to find a job, one of the first orders of business was to craft a name suitable for a resume. To support the illusion that he was a man with a separate body and mind, they would need to construct the kind of moniker that such a person would have. Since neither of them could remember being that person, and because they hadn't acquired the laptop yet, this was a job for the library.

And so, before dawn one morning, they struggled their twin half-bodies into a single set of clothes, hobbled to the nearest branch, and waited for it to open. The librarian they spoke to was only mildly alarmed by their appearance, having just started his work day securing medical help for a man who had a seizure in the front vestibule.

"W'hee wyanth to lyearn aboubt namesh," the brothers said in measured tandem.

The librarian nodded, scratching absently at the stubble he hadn't had time to shave. "Names, okay. Any specific kind? Or are we looking at history, meanings of names, that sort of thing?"

"Norm'mall names," said the brothers.

"Normal as in common?"

Left gave a thumbs-up. It was less stressful than both of them trying to nod at the same time.

The man showed them how to log in on one of the public computers and gave them some coaching on how to research the most common baby names from different periods and regions. They thanked him, and he busied himself helping two high school kids find a graphic novel they couldn't remember anything about, except what color the cover was.

The brothers pored over every list of names they could find. There were lists by country, by ethnicity, indexesthat included each name's meaning based on etymology. Names, it turned out, had always been conceived as protective shells encasing the people to whom they were given. Names given to children by parents expressed their wishes for the children to develop certain personality traits, the spiritual protection of God or their ancestors; names given by adults to themselves were meant to portray the nature of the person's true character, reinforcing it through repetition each time the name was written or spoken. Perhaps most relevant, they found, was the tradition of superhero "secret identities," which were there to obscure the person's true nature, rather than reinforce it.

"Remember, we're making up a fake name," Left said when Right began to worry about the consequences if he chose the wrong name for himself. "It's not about who you are, it's about who you want the people who do the hiring to think you are."

"Who do I want them to think I am?" said Right.

"Somebody who could be anybody," said Left. "Someone who shows up and works a job and does okay at it and goes home. Not somebody ambitious, or threatening. Not the life of the party."

They had gathered that European names were the most common, even among people not of European descent, so they looked at those exclusively. Right liked Allen, especially when they learned that it meant "handsome," but Left rejected the idea.

"You don't want people to think you're handsome," he said. "Normal people aren't handsome."

"Yeah, well, they look better than us," said Right.

Left chuckled; in those early days, it came out as a breathy sputtering, almost like a sneeze.

With his brother's guidance, Right refined the list of possibilities according to which ones had to do with twins, brotherhood, safety, humility. They looked up instructions on how to format a resume, concocted an education and work history for "Thomas J. Williams," and set about applying for the most anonymous drudge work they could find. Right fantasized about working at a pet store, but he had to admit that his appearance would probably scare the animals as well as the customers. It made sense to look for something more private, with as few people as possible required to look at him on a daily basis, and from there it became clear that a call center job would be the easiest way to go. He had an interview scheduled by the time they left the library.

Going home was a more complicated process than the pre-dawn walk. They had to work out a labyrinthine route through side streets and alleyways to avoid too many curious onlookers, working off directions on scrap paper.

The journey gave Right plenty of time to reflect on his new identity. He had known, going in, that this adventure was going to culminate in a new name, a shield of normalcy to hide his deformity from the world he sought to join. What he didn't expect was to feel so disturbed by it. Why should he? The name was just words on paper. It didn't have anything to do with who he was, any more than the clothes he used to cover himself or the crutch Left used to help them walk. And yet it was there, just the same: a feeling of loss, as if he were somehow diminished by typing those words and sending them out into the world. The name felt more false than the previous jobs they'd made up, or the associate's degree he didn't have.

They toasted that night with wine shoplifted from the

corner store. The bottle had been coated in a film of dust when they found it, leading them to wonder if the cashier had seen them tuck it into their coat and elected to let it go. The contents were too sweet for either of their taste, but they didn't complain. It was the ritual that felt important, not the particulars. Marking occasions felt all the more urgent then, having had so few to mark.

"To Thomas J. Williams," Left said, raising his glass over the pasta and salad that remained of dinner. "Long may he reign."

Right forced a grin and raised his own glass, avoiding eye contact with his brother. Years later, he would look back and identify this moment as the first concrete warning sign, and still more years after that, he would wonder if it had ever really happened at all. But back then, living through it in real time, he could only think to write off the unease he felt as anxiety about getting a job, leaving his brother alone for half the day, needing to keep up a pretense the entire time with the coworkers he was about to have. The unease never quite went away, but over time he grew used to it, until he was able to content himself that surely everyone must live with this same discomfort as the background noise of everything they say and do on the outside. A nameless, creeping fear that must be constantly silenced just to move about the world the way a person is supposed to.

"To, uh . . . to me," said Right. "Long may I endure."

Left, too, would come to look back on this moment and realize that he should have known. Right's quiet, passive refusal to use the name at home that they, themselves, had chosen for him could never have boded well. Both of them, in retrospect, had known that something was off kilter about the toast. The only thing they disagreed about—never knowingly, never explicitly—was what the wrong thing was, and what should be done about it. Whether it should be fought, or fixed, or fled from. Whether it was fundamentally about a failure to agree on everything, or an insistence on it.

That night, Left dreamed that he pulled up the carpet in the motel room and found a trap door underneath. He opened the door, called down into the concrete pit beneath it, and felt, more than heard, another voice call out in response, with a blast of cold wind on his face and a colder chill seeping into his ears.

Right dreamed of a huge, red bird with the face of a man removing the organs from his body cavity, appraising them quietly, turning each one around in his hand before packing it into a suitcase at his feet. All except his brain, which the bird-man swallowed down in a single gulp, and there the dream ended.

They both awoke with an ache in their bones and assumed it was from the long walk.

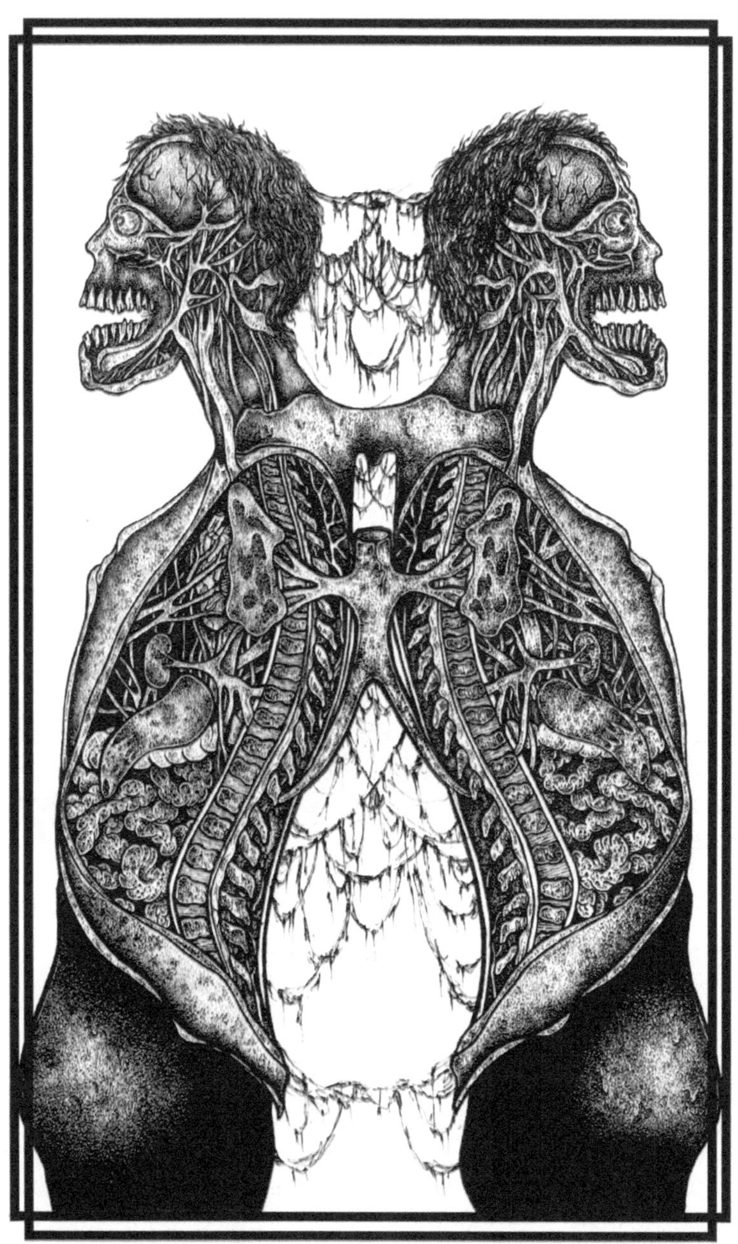

What was, moments ago, a human cadaver bisected to display a cross-section, has become two men with half a body, lit suddenly by the heat of consciousness, newborn in their decrepitude.

CHAPTER 2

"Heart" means "the center of everything"

THE LUMPS BENEATH their skin become growths. At first, it looks disturbing. Their skin stretches across these new protrusions like a drum, straining, aching, until the flesh can grow to accommodate its new territory. As new organs fill in behind the skin, they begin to look and feel, if not less gruesome, then at least hopeful of one day looking in the mirror and seeing something that resembles the rest of society.

When Left awakens one morning to find that he finished growing his chin during the night, the brothers dip into their fun money for a bottle of scotch. Left gets it from the liquor store while Right is at work, and they celebrate that evening after dining on a grocery store rotisserie chicken. Each of them eats half: one leg, one thigh, one breast, one wing. They wash it down with the scotch, warm and earthy, like submerging their brains in a hot spring.

They break the wishbone. Left gets the bigger half. "I wish for my brother to grow a chin next," he says, pleased with the idea of this being the way of things: for him to lead the way, and Right to follow, traveling safely in his brother's footsteps. They toast the wish, each one raising his plastic motel cup.

Right is amazed at how fast the surface of the scotch in the bottle descends. Compares it, internally, to formaldehyde draining from a cadaver. He looks at the chicken bones on his plate. I am like this chicken, he thinks, grinning at something Left has said. In the spirit of the moment, he pours out his cup on top of the bones.

Left chuckles. "What did you do that for?"

"It's you," says Right.

"The hell are you talking about?" says Left. "It's a bunch of chicken bones, covered in scotch."

"It's a me-ta-phor." Right pokes his finger into the tabletop with each syllable. "Of course it's not *literally* you, but it's *like* you, see? Half a dead body, full of preservative fluid."

Left pouts.

"Get it?" says Right.

Left shushes him. With a new chin changing the architecture of his mouth, it comes with a generous helping of spittle. "I get it all right," he says. "It's insulting. Would you like it if I compared you to a dead bird?"

Right realizes his error, and realizes that he has realized it later than he ideally should, and then combines these two realizations to realize that he is drunk. "I didn't mean it as an insult."

"Is that supposed to matter?" says Left.

Right wants to say that it should, but he suspects this wouldn't make things any better. Instead, he reaches for the half-ribcage on his plate and lifts it a few inches above the table. In his hand, the clean-picked chicken breast walks on invisible legs, across to Left's plate. "I'm sorry I said something wrong," he says in a tiny puppet-voice, bobbing the ribcage up and down with each word. "What I meant was that I'm glad we're alive and have each other, and I want to be your brother forever and ever!"

Left cracks a smile and picks up the ribcage from his own plate. "Okay," his half-chicken says, "but it's your turn to do the dishes tonight!"

It is not, in fact, Right's turn to do the dishes, but he decides to accept it as the price of calming things down. "You've got a deal," says his half-chicken, and returns to its place on his own plate. He rises from his seat and collects their plates.

Right is beginning to recognize the chord struck deep in his gut by Left's displeasure. Despite them being cut from the same cloth, there is a dissonance between them. Each seeks to move through the world in subtly different ways, but only his brother seems to have a problem with this. Right wonders if there is something wrong with him for not feeling the same resistance, but he cannot wrap his mind around Left's perspective, no matter how he tries. After all, their existence began with them being cleft apart. What is the purpose of one self becoming two, if not to allow each to go his own way?

"Tell me about the cottage again," says Left.

"What about it?" says Right, rinsing a day's worth of cutlery all grouped together in one hand.

"Just walk me through it again. Start with the front door."

"Haven't we already had that conversation?"

"Yeah, but I'm drunk now," says Left. "And you're the one with the imagination anyway. That's how it works, right? The left brain is for logic and the right brain is for creativity?"

Right has read up on this himself. It's called lateralized specialization, and doesn't actually have much to do with logic *or* creativity, but he indulges his brother anyway. "The front door is weathered, thick oak, but with a small window in the center, and sidelights. Inside is a foyer, where—"

"I don't want to do the foyer this time," says Left. "What about the living room?"

"First door on the right after you walk in," says Right. "It has one huge window that faces south, so that plenty of sunlight can warm the house in the winter. The stone hearth is across from the window. There's a television in the corner, but we're too far out in the woods to get any channels, so it's just connected to a DVD player. Each of us has our own easy chair, yours in brown leather, mine in green, and both of them recline so that we can nap, or lay back and look all around the room: to the window, to the TV, to the art on the split timber walls, where we'll put all the wildlife paintings we collect. There's two more doors besides the one to the foyer, one to the dining room and one to the kitchen, where you can see the huge brick oven where we bake our—"

"Brick oven?" Left interrupts, and Right realizes, again too late, that he's thinking of his own separate version of the cottage, not the one they work on together.

"I just thought of it," says Right. "Against the back wall, so the smoke vents outside. It looks old fashioned, but we can make amazing bread in it."

"I'm not sure how I feel about this," says Left. "Go back to the way we talked about it before."

"I . . . I can't remember all of it right now," says Right. "I'm drunk too, after all."

"So drunk that you can't remember our cottage?" says Left. "*I'm* drunk too and *I* can remember it perfectly. The kitchen should have a floor of red tile, the color of brick. Have you forgotten that too?"

Right still has no heart, yet he can feel something pulsing angrily within him. Not for the first time, he wonders how it is that the blood moves through his body, and whether he can even be considered human, lacking the organ whose very name places it at the center of everything.

Unaware of Left's etymological research, he has been doing some of his own. He knows that "heart" refers to much more than just circulation. For millennia, it has been equated with thoughts, feelings like courage and affection, even the soul itself. The heart is the seat of everything. Without the heart, the body dies. And yet he lives, regardless. He suspects it is only Left's proximity and good will that keep him alive. Good will that he can't seem to stop offending.

Desperate, Right rotates the cutlery in his hand and runs his thumb along the blade of a steak knife, pressing it hard into the skin. He screams, his elbow crashing hard onto the edge of the sink. The serrated edge made it more painful than he expected.

"Right!" his brother shouts.

"I'm fine." Right grips the sink with his palm and pushes himself upright. A trickle of blood runs down the edge.

"You're bleeding," says Left.

"I think I must be a little too drunk," Right says distantly. Hearing his brother's disappointment replaced by concern, the anxious pulsing in him subsides. All of a sudden, he barely feels the pain.

Left stands and hops over to the sink. "Make sure to wash out the dirt. After that, we should get you to bed. I'll take care of the rest of the dishes."

He helps Right into the bedroom, all the while tormenting himself with the suspicion that he somehow caused the injury by distracting his brother with talk of the cottage. He reminds himself that Right can only think about so many things at once, not having the logical side of the brain.

"Sorry about the cut," he says, slipping his arm out from under Right as Right reclines on the bed.

"I know," says Right. "It's okay." He is only half-aware of himself saying this, bombarded as he is by the cocktail of feelings taking root inside him. Embarrassment, for forgetting which version of the cottage was which, and fear of the consequences; resentment, for Left's overreaction, and shame at himself for resenting it; and, underneath it all, gratitude for his brother's concern and the comfort he gets from the starchy softness of the motel bed. He's not used to feeling so much at once.

Left leaves to finish the dishes while Right holds his bloody thumb, wrapped in a washcloth, tightly inside his fist. By the time left comes back, the wound has closed.

"Good," says Left. "You know, I got to thinking while I was in there. Maybe having one of those big stone ovens wouldn't be such a bad thing."

Right nods, mainly because he still suspects that's the most he can get away with, without triggering Left's imaginative jealousy. "It's not something we need. Just forget I mentioned it, I don't know what I was thinking."

"And then, I don't know why, but that reminded me . . . " Left takes a seat in the chair across from the bed. It's unclear to Right whether his brother heard what he said. "Do you ever wonder, what if we're not actually growing out our own bodies, but getting ready to split again?"

Between the alcohol and the bleeding, Right feels fatigue creeping in behind his eyes. "What? Like in the morgue where we first woke up?"

"What if," Left continues, "when we've filled out completely, a huge saw comes along and cuts each of us down the middle, and each of us had a new brother, and then there would be four of us?"

A chill overtakes Right, not entirely born from his own tiredness. A hundred metal W's parade behind his eyes. He can feel Lincoln watching from somewhere just out of view, nodding as if in confirmation of something he's said. "Well, uh . . . that's a novel idea," says Right.

"I know!" says Left. "Just thinking about it makes me so sad and worried, because what if you liked your new half better than you liked me, and you only wanted to spend time with him? And what if I tried to do the same with my new other half, but we didn't get along so well, and ended up hating each other, and then I was totally alone?"

Right remains silent. He cannot reconcile the excitement in Left's voice with the things he's expressing. He wonders if his brother is going insane.

"God, wouldn't that be horrible?" says Left.

"Yeah, but you sound so happy about it."

"I'm not!" says Left. "I don't know why. I've got all these thoughts running wild inside me, like my own mind is on a treadmill, and I'm struggling to keep from falling off, and it keeps going faster and faster, Right, it's so fast! I can't keep up with myself!"

"Why? What's going on?" says Right.

"I don't know," says Left. "Just thinking about all this stuff is putting me on edge. I mean it doesn't feel like I'm imagining it, you know? It's more like a memory. A bad one."

Right feels an urge forming in his gut. Something in him wants to tell his brother about Lincoln. Right is afraid of the urge, especially because he feels it so physically, as if what little body he has were betraying itself over this secret. But, hearing all this, it's almost as if Left knows the secret already, and in that case wouldn't it serve Right better to be honest? Unless it's a coincidence, in which case bringing it up could be a huge mistake. Yet more feelings flood his body. He can't stop imagining scenarios where he tells, and Left is disgusted and angry at how deceitful he's been, the way he's betrayed their brotherhood in his thoughts again and again, and so he keeps his mouth shut.

"I'm getting the rest of the scotch," says Left. "I think it might help me slow down a little."

"I could go for some more myself," says Right. For a moment, he considers mentioning something he has thought about often: that someone must have cut them in half at some point, and they have no idea who did this, or who they were when they were a single body, or why they came to life in the way they did, but Left is already out of the room before he can decide whether to say anything.

By the time Left returns, Right is asleep. He thinks he'll be able to finish the scotch by himself. He sits on the bed, takes another swig, sets the bottle on the end table, and passes out briefly. He wakes a few minutes later, finishes the bottle, and falls into a much deeper sleep, untroubled by the thoughts of loss and abandonment he sought to escape. There is something warming about the experience of being drunk. It's a warmth that comes without strength or vigor, but that's its charm. It's the warmth of helplessness. A deep surrender that can be had for a half-hour's wages at a time.

***

When Left wakes the next day, Right is already out of bed. He feels so weak, he can barely lift his head, which is no surprise; the only surprise is that he's managed to get up before the sun, as the dimness of the light coming in through the window suggests. "Right?" he groans. Then, louder, "Right!"

Right appears in the doorway, fully clothed. "You're finally awake."

"Finally?" Left looks at the clock on the end table, which reads 6:42.

"It's almost night," says Right.

Left lets out another sustained groan. "I slept all day?"

"You had a lot to drink," says Right.

"We both did, but you're up."

"You want some food?" says Right. "I can put something in the microwave, I think. Or get some takeout, we can afford it."

"No we can't," says Left. "I'm the one who does our budget, you know that."

Right doesn't respond. He knows they can afford it, but it's better if Left doesn't know his brother has been checking his work on their finances.

"My body feels heavy," says Left. "I know I should eat, but I also don't want to be awake right now. Everything hurts."

"Well, I've heard that's a thing that happens when you've got a hangover," says Right. "I'll grab you a glass of water, at least. Can you sit up?"

"I'll try."

Right heads for the kitchen, and Left struggles onto his elbow, then scoots backward to prop his back against the headboard. The whole process feels wrong, as if there's a sack of rocks tethered to his hip. He throws off the covers and screams.

Lying on the bed next to his leg is another leg. An entire leg, attached to his body, but nothing like the one he is used to. This one is pale, its skin translucent, displaying the web of veins and tendons beneath. Touching it sends a bolt of pain through his bones, especially the new ones, and leaves his finger tacky with plasma.

Right crashes into the room, pushing the door open with his shoulder as his foot comes down from a hop. He, too, screams.

"What is this thing?" says Left.

"Looks like a leg," says Right.

"No. This," Left pats his original leg, "is a leg. This other thing looks like a very big, ugly fish that is trying to eat me from the waist up."

"Can you move it?"

"No, but it hurts something awful." He gives it another experimental poke and finds that it's exactly as painful as last time.

"It's a right leg," Right points out.

"Miracle of miracles."

"And I also notice you've got an entire, uh . . . "

"That too." Left frowns at the small appendage between his leg and the new, offending leg. "Is that what it's supposed to look like?"

"I would not be the one to ask," says Right.

"Well, at least it doesn't hurt as much as the leg-thing does," says Left. "I wonder how this is going to change things."

"The whole leg seriously grew overnight?" says Right.

"I don't get how it happened."

"Was it the scotch?" says Right. "I found the empty bottle on the night stand, you must have had a lot. Or is it because you're the one with the heart?"

"I've never read anything to suggest that either of those causes an extra limb to grow in your sleep," says Left. "I just hope it gets, uh, finished. Walking would be cool, but I'd prefer hopping over having to drag this thing around for the rest of my life. And it's so painful, Right, you can't imagine."

"I guess I can't," Right mutters. He shakes his head. "Whole-ass leg!"

"I might not be able to do the housework for a while."

"Of course," says Right. "What will we do if it never starts working like it should?"

"Cut it off, I guess. And hope the same thing doesn't happen to you."

"We can't cut it off!" says Right. "It's a leg!"

"We can and we will, if it comes to that," says Left. "But we don't know yet. We'll figure it out if it becomes a problem."

"I'm really sorry about this, Left."

Left shrugs. "You didn't do anything."

"But I'm sorry. I know I didn't do anything, it just, I feel like I'm supposed to be sorry anyway? To—I don't know, you know what I'm talking about, right? That this shouldn't have happened?"

Left frowns. "Thanks. I know I just woke up, but I'm really tired."

"Go back to sleep," says Right. "It makes sense to be tired. Growing is hard work."

"That's what I hear," says Left. He is asleep again almost as soon as the last word leaves his mouth.

Right sits at the table. He wishes they had more scotch, so he could find out if it might make him grow a leg too, but he also doesn't ever want to drink as much of it as it looks like Left did, so he supposes he'll never know. It's hard to imagine that it really had anything to do with what happened, but then, he would never have imagined Left growing an entire leg in a single night, and here they are.

He allows Lincoln to enter the room and sit across the table from him.

"Left has another leg," he tells his imaginary twin. "A right leg."

"I saw," says Lincoln. "Are you jealous?"

"I don't know," says Right. "I guess? I wish I had two legs."

"But it's not even a good looking leg," says Lincoln. "It's hideous. And it doesn't work."

"But he has it," says Right.

"It's better to have no leg than that thing that's attached to your brother. He said so himself." Lincoln tosses his hair dismissively. "Look at me. I only have one leg, and I'm fine. Better than fine. I'm imaginary."

Right understands, intellectually, that Lincoln's remark was a joke intended to cheer him up, but Lincoln is too self-absorbed to think about the fact that Right isn't imaginary, nor does he have a second leg. The worst of both worlds. He could be anything if he were imaginary, but he has to settle for reality and do what he can with the resources he's got. "Do you want another leg?" he asks Lincoln.

"Never. I'm happy just the way I am. And you should be too."

"Even if I never grow again? If this is all I'll ever be?"

"You can grow as much as you want," says Lincoln. "You only have so much control over how much of that growth takes place in your physical body, but the limitations of biology will never match the ones imposed by the mind."

"What the hell is that supposed to mean?" says Right.

"It means that regardless of how your body does or doesn't develop, you'll never leave this motel room if you don't let yourself," says Lincoln. "It means you'll never have a name that's yours. One day you'll realize you're an old man, and for all your years on Earth, you've known so little that you might as well have lived that life as a caged hamster."

"I leave the motel room every day to go to work," says Right.

"And come back here right after," says Lincoln. "You really never wonder if there's more to you than him?"

"Left needs my help."

"Left needs help," Lincoln agrees. "But it doesn't have to be from you. You can't even provide the most crucial parts of it."

"Yeah, yeah, I know, I'm not my brother's keeper."

"He wants to be yours, though," says Lincoln.

Right frowns. When he first met Lincoln, the imaginary twin was something between a role model and a rival. The hardest thing about interacting with him was balancing the feelings of resentment with the drive to be more like him. Tonight, though, something else has crept in around the edges. Lincoln feels more like a peer. Right suspects that a big part of his pushiness is coming from Lincoln's jealousy of Right's ability to grow at all. It's almost pathetic. Lincoln may be handsomer, and more confident, and maybe even better at being half a person, but he will never change. Right may have grown only by little, staggering bits, but Lincoln looks just the same as he did the night Right first imagined him.

Without another word, Right leaves Lincoln sitting at the table and goes to check on his sleeping brother. He and Left look more different now than they ever have, maybe more than they ever will. The unconscious man in the bed almost appears to be a stranger, when Right looks closely enough at the finer points of his features. If they're not careful, he thinks, they may indeed be strangers to each other, eventually.

That must be why there's so much angst between them, sometimes. They both want to be more than just two men living in a motel room, more than just the sum of their parts. That's why everything needs to be so controlled. It's a fine line between growing together and growing apart. Is it really so bad to want togetherness?

interlude

"Family" means "servants of the house"

ALL PEOPLE, at one time or another, are presented with things that seem impossible. Some more than others, of course, and it does not get easier over time. For those who have already lived through the impossible, the appearance of this new thing often seems all the more incredible. After all, they have been through the hardship of seeing things for what they really are, come to terms with them, and therefore should be done with the process, only to now be forced to edit their reality once more, shrinking themselves further and further inside an expanding and ever more chaotic universe.

Wise people often claim to value being humbled in this way, but only because they have the luxury of choosing it. The human mind is a fragile thing, only equipped to grapple with the unknown when it is contained in the most familiar frame possible. That's the principle behind everything they've created for themselves: language, science, mathematics, and, most of all, storytelling.

Once upon a time, in a forest in the foothills much like this one—and some would even say it *was* this one—there lived a family of two within a house of four. One was a boy with no hands, having lost his in an accident during his birth. The other was his elder brother, who had two hands and had used them to care for the younger boy since they were little children.

The other two people in the house were the boys' parents. They were cruel and neglectful, their hearts calcified by decades of pressure from the developers who wanted their land. They, and their parents, and their parents' parents had lived in the forest since the colonizers built their first crude, wooden shacks there. After the bombs fell and the war-men came home with pockets full of spoils and hearts full of bottomless, unyielding hunger, then came the highway, and with it the motorcars, and the resort towns, and the subdivisions. Every year in the household became a ledger dictating how many parts of themselves the parents would have to cut off in order to keep up with the rising property taxes and cost of keeping them all fed.

As much as this dragged them down, they would not consider leaving the house to find a new home. The house had always been theirs, and therefore it should always be theirs. They could not imagine living anywhere else.

Though they made effort to trim all the available fat from their budget, they could not find a way to cut off their sons. They resented the boys, who manifested the heftiest line of the ledger, and the only thing that diluted their resentment was their indifference to the younger son's suffering.

And so, the elder brother became the one to bring the younger brother his medicine and meals, remind the parents of doctor appointments, and, in time, the one who drove the brother wherever he needed to go. When he came of age, the parents stopped letting him use their car, so he had to get a job in the nearest resort town and scrape together enough money to buy his own. It barely ran, a rusted-out old pickup that could stop and go and not much else, but it was what needed to be done. This way the younger boy could still be together with his brother, whom he loved, despite all their troubles.

The boys grew up, but never left the house in the woods; the younger one could not, and the elder one could not imagine wanting to. The parents grew old and eventually died, leaving the brothers behind in the little house where they'd lived their whole lives. For the elder brother, this meant things could finally start to improve. The house had always been his, in a sense, by right of being the one who took care of it. Now it was his completely, without the burden of his resentful ancestors holding him back. Money was always tight, but the elder man worked hard so that his brother could live. And this, for him, was enough.

For the younger brother, the situation had not changed in any significant way. He might not feel compelled any longer to stay in his bedroom, to hide himself from the eyes of parents who didn't want to be reminded of him, but moving freely about the house didn't feel much different. It was nothing more than a slightly larger room to be trapped in. The woods were not a good place for him.

He begged the elder brother to consider moving them somewhere with more people and more services, where he might be able to lead a life that felt merely repressed, rather than completely smothered, but the brother wouldn't hear it. They were barely making it out there in the countryside. Surely they would never be able to support themselves in the city. Lacking any way to rebut this idea, the younger brother remained trapped there, held hostage by the only person in the world who had the opportunity to love him.

It might appear, to an outside observer, that the younger brother had no recourse but to resign himself to a life of benevolent dependency. What an outside observer might not take into account is that there are other people in the world than humans. The brothers' ancestors, back in the log cabin days, had handed down stories of the Other Folk who had shared their land, stories that survived in some form until the brothers' time. As children, they had always assumed the Other Folk to be Native Americans. As adults, they had noticed certain inconsistencies in the versions they heard— Native Americans did not live underground or inside of trees, after all, and you could not make one of them serve you by invoking their true name—but they had written this off as the kind of embellishment that comes naturally with tall tales.

Desperation, however, is a powerful motivator.

One day the brothers quarreled, in more or less their usual way, with the younger brother shouting *let me be* at one wall, and the elder brother shouting *let me protect you* at the opposite wall, neither one of them really addressing the other. This time, though, it ended with the younger one stalking out of the house and into the woods. The elder heard the sounds of footsteps through fallen leaves grow fainter and fainter, until he could no longer make them out.

He could not understand what had made his brother so angry. After all, he had spent his entire life attending to him, keeping their house in order, working tirelessly so that his brother could eat and sleep safely. Well, he said to himself, sooner or later he'll have to realize that we need each other and come back. It's not like he could go far without the benefit of hands, anyway.

When night fell and the younger brother had not yet returned, the elder finally gave into his feelings of guilt, put on his coat, and went into the woods with a flashlight to find him. Having grown up in the woods, he knew how to follow a trail, but even so, the younger brother's was difficult to make out. There were footprints in the dirt at the back of the house, but they grew more sporadic as he progressed, and branched out in many different directions as he ventured farther into the thickets.

One trail led to a clearing where the younger brother had apparently paced around in a circle for some time, but there was no other trail leading off from the circle where he might have gone after. Another trail dead-ended in front of an ancient oak that looked almost 100 feet tall. Another time, the elder brother traced a series of winding detours up and down a hillside for a full hour before he realized that he was following his own footprints, and couldn't figure out when he'd lost his brother's trail in favor of his own. There was simply no concrete sign of where he had gone.

The authorities were no help. They couldn't follow a trail that didn't exist any more than the elder brother could. And so, once the questions were questioned and the reports were reported, he was forced to look into different ways of finding his brother. Older ways. He, too, had heard the stories of the Other Folk. Most of those stories were cautionary tales that warned against seeking their help. But after all, desperation is a powerful motivator.

The elder brother didn't know the true name of any of the Other Folk, but he did remember other details from the stories. In one of them, some settlers had built their house on top of a hill, not knowing that the Other Folk lived underneath it. As long as they lived there, the family was tormented by visitors who showed up inside their house without ever coming in through the door.

Someone they had never seen before would walk up and seat himself at the dinner table with them, help himself to as much food as he wanted, talk about the weather and the harvest as if he were part of the family himself, and then walk out of the room and disappear. The children would say their prayers before bed, only to look up and see another child sleeping there. Household items would fly from shelves as if suddenly imbued with life, or vanish completely and be replaced with strange baubles made of wood and coal.

In the story, the settlers made a pact with the Other Folk. The husband built a doorway, frame and all, and installed it in the floor of the cellar. The Other Folk could come and go through the door as they pleased, and the family would leave things there for them to take: food, newspapers, toys, and whatever else they could think of. In return, the Other Folk would not interpose themselves in the family's affairs, make use of the house as if it were their own, or terrorize the settlers in any way. In the story, they mostly stuck to this agreement, but not always. After all, if they always kept their promises exactly, then there would be no more stories.

Taking a cue from this story, the elder brother built a

door. He placed it in the floor of his own cellar. He waited a week, but nothing happened. So, he opened the door himself and started digging. When the hole was deep enough for him to stand in it and have the door frame circle his waist, he hit bedrock, but he didn't stop. He fetched a mattock and kept going.

If you search long enough, you will eventually find something. It may not be the thing you were looking for, but the longer you've been at it, the easier it is to convince yourself that whatever you've found will have to do.

One day, the elder brother awoke to find a man he had never seen before standing at the foot of his bed.

"All right," said the man, "you've got my attention."

The elder brother leaped from his bed and immediately knelt at the strange man's feet. He was relieved and terrified at once, knowing that the Other Folk must be the ones who had taken his brother, and could surely take him as well. With one of them here, though, he could at least negotiate, which he knew from the stories must be his only hope of ever seeing his brother again. He begged the man to tell him where the younger brother had gone, and what he had to do to get him back.

The man shook his head. The younger brother had left the house of his own free will, and it was not the place of this Other man to bring him back in captivity. He could give the elder brother the tools he might need, but as for actually finding the younger brother and getting him to return, the elder would have to do that himself. He would have to understand why his sibling had left in order to bring him back.

"But how can I understand if he's not here for me to ask?" the elder brother protested.

The Other man smiled. He could make a new younger brother, cut from the same cloth. Normally it would be impossible without the parents alive, but it could be done, if the elder brother were willing to make the proper sacrifices.

"What sacrifices would those be?" the elder brother asked without hesitation. He was sure there was nothing he wouldn't do to help his sibling.

The Other man told him: to make a person—a real one—you need to give him a mind and a body. It would be like growing a house plant from a cutting. The elder brother would give enough mind, enough body to craft the spell, and then he would find himself with a second chance to understand his brother's motives.

The elder brother agreed, of course. Another chance was exactly what he needed. Whatever had made his brother leave had surely been a misunderstanding, one that he could correct if only he were given the opportunity, and here the opportunity was. After all, each of them was all the other had. They were family, closer than family, inseparable but for this horrible mishap that had taken the younger brother away.

And so the Other man sharpened his saw, a fierce instrument as long as he was tall, with hundreds of W-teeth forming a vast, predatory smile, with a matching smile on the man's face all the while. It unsettled the elder brother, but he knew he had to do what was necessary. This had to be put right. It *would* be put right. Even with the magical strangeness of the disappearance, and the entry of the Other man into his home, he knew that their reconciliation had to be inevitable. For all the impossible things that seemed to be happening anyway, for the brothers to lose each other was impossibility on another level. It was the one thing he was unwilling to question, the one impossible thing that he could never imagine proving otherwise.

That's the thing about the impossible, though. It always exists outside of what you understand, always invisible until it is staring you in the face, too late to be anticipated. But it is still there, hanging in the air, waiting for the chance to reveal itself. Inevitable as entropy. Tugging at the threads of the universe, in need only of the right person on the other end to tug back.

CHAPTER 3

"Apartment" means "a separated place"

AS HIS NEW leg heals, Left sleeps almost constantly for weeks. The motel room grows untidy, and their bank account drains with the cost of prepared meals that Right has to pick up on the way home from work. When he's awake, Left eats voraciously but takes no pleasure in it. Mostly he groans and demands as many painkillers as he can safely take. His skin fades to a grayish color and his face takes on a sunken look, but Right doesn't dare seek out a doctor for his brother. How would he explain his condition? How would he explain anything about either of them?

The only thing he can do is pick up more overtime shifts at work, so that they don't run out of money while praying to whatever force has animated them for Left's recovery. Once Right gets permission from his boss, he starts working 7 days a week. He's exhausted all the time, and shorter than usual with the people on the other end of his phone calls, but at least Left is rarely awake to see it.

In his darker moments, which are increasingly frequent as the weeks pass, he wonders if he has made himself a slave to someone who is already dead. But what choice does he have?

Lincoln doesn't exactly provide any help in alleviating these worries. The imaginary twin shows up more and more often as time progresses, at work and at home. Right supposes he does need someone to talk to, he just wishes it could be someone a bit less critical.

"What good is all this work if you never get to enjoy what you earn?" Lincoln asks during their lunch break one day.

"I'm just making sure our needs are met." Right shifts his weight in the bucket seat so he's facing away from Lincoln. Lately, he has been eating lunch in the car, since he can't seem to avoid talking to someone who nobody else can see.

"*Our* needs?" says Lincoln. Right can practically feel the imaginary breath on the back of his neck. "It only really seems like one person's needs matter in this arrangement."

"I need food and a place to sleep too," Right grumbles.

"And that means you have to work yourself to the bone? Just for those basic necessities?"

"What do you want me to do about it?" he snaps.

"Calm down," says Lincoln. "I don't want you to do anything, I just want you to view your situation through a clearer lens. There's nothing wrong with you wanting to help your brother, but let's call it what it is."

"And what's that?"

"A parasitic relationship," says Lincoln.

"Get out," says Right.

"I'm only—"

"Get *out!*" he shouts, and Lincoln doesn't appear for several days. When he returns, he no longer brings up Left's condition at all.

Then, one day, Right comes home and finds his twin walking stiffly around the kitchenette on both legs. Without saying anything, he hobbles over and gives Left a close, one-armed hug.

"Things can get back to normal now," says Left.

"Thank goodness," says Right. "That's all I've been hoping for this whole time."

"Me too," says Left.

The new leg heals, but the skin looks rumpled and discolored, like a burn scar, and he limps if he stays on his feet for too long. Left never quite grows to love the new limb. In fact, he complains about it daily. Seeing his disappointment,

Right almost hopes he never grows a second leg. How will Left feel if his brother gets a normal, fully working leg when he is stuck with the one that grew in too fast?

Months pass, bringing comfortable tedium but no answer to the question. Right's left arm comes in before the leg, leading to a few months of uncomfortable top-heaviness that requires him to learn new ways of using the crutch. Left barely responds to any of this. He doesn't express delight or anger at any anatomical milestone. There are no more celebratory chickens or bottles, largely because Left no longer seems to find any of the process worth celebrating and Right doubts it would be worth the trouble to ask why. It takes nearly two years, but in time, both of them acquire a more or less normative human body.

Once there is enough of him that he feels safe going out, Left insists on getting a job himself, feeling the need to finally contribute in ways that go beyond just cooking meals. The first and only place he applies is the same call center where Right works, where he presents himself as Thomas J. Williams' brother, Thomas A. Williams. The illusion is not so hard to pull off. The body they came from did not have a perfectly symmetrical face to begin with, and the differences in their appearance became more pronounced as each one grew out. Ultimately, they appear as two men, close together in age, clearly blood relatives, but not identical.

He gets the job. Every day they drive, together, to the office where they sit side-by-side, in separate, matching cubicles. They spend their days having the same series of conversations with the people on the other side of their headsets. They don't interact much while they're there, but they are always together. A few times a day, Left puts his hand to the cubicle wall he shares with his brother. He convinces himself that Right is doing the same thing on the other side, and that he can feel their hands almost touching through the barrier.

For Right, the changes over time that result from his own

body filling out are more personal, not something to be shared between the two of them as much as Left's. His new limbs come in slower, and while they do make life easier, the change in his ability isn't as drastic. He goes back to his normal work schedule.

Left resumes all of the household chores. Doing the cooking and housework while also holding a job is stressful, but anytime Right brings this up, his brother insists on keeping his household duties, as if he needs to prove how much he can handle. Right, in turn, insists on always being the one to drive the car. He isn't fully sure why he does this. It's not even a very time-consuming responsibility, but he feels like something, at least, should be his, if they're going to be laying claim to their days in this way.

The real change for him—the one he doesn't discuss with Left—is the one that happens the first day he feels a faint heartbeat behind the developing half of his rib cage. It's weak and stammering, at first, an incomplete organ struggling to do its whole job without its whole corpus, which is something Right feels he can empathize with. But it grows quickly, filling in all the space it can as soon as it's available, as though the heart were desperate to be complete, filling itself out with the urgency of a firefighter charging into a burning building. And this, too, is something Right finds familiar: this desperation to be complete, to be fully alive at last.

The fact that he never discusses the heart with his brother is not exactly a decision he makes at any point. It's more like a conspicuous lack of a decision at every juncture where it might come up. There never seems to be a good time. He knows, instinctively, that it's one of those topics that must be brought to Left carefully and in the right light, lest it excite his brother's discomfort. For some reason, Left always seems comforted by the idea that he has something Right doesn't have, and Right knows instinctively that there's going to be a lot of mental massaging to do around the fact that it's no longer the case. The opportunity to start that massaging never quite presents itself, so he simply goes on not talking about it, and Left goes on not asking.

Maybe it's the insistence of the new organ propelling the blood through his veins, but Right does begin feeling the desire to claim something more for himself. He doesn't bring the heart up with Lincoln either, but he does find a topic more to the imaginary twin's liking. He tells Lincoln about how they chose the name Thomas for him, and the constant, background discomfort he has felt about it ever since. And Lincoln, to his credit, has helpful suggestions. For a few days, anytime Right is alone, he brainstorms possibilities with Lincoln until they arrive at an agreement, which Lincoln forces him to bring before Left as soon as he can.

"I'm thinking of calling myself something else," Right says on the drive home one day. He has to keep eyes on the road while driving, which forces any conversation he has to be half-attentive, casual by necessity, and he hopes this will make the discussion easier.

"Something else? What do you mean?" says Left. "You mean at work, or at home?"

"Both," says Right. "I don't need to be Right anymore. It's not accurate. I'm more than just the right side of a body."

"But you were the right side, originally."

"So?"

Left shrugs, a bit too dramatically to come off as casual as he means it. "I just think it's important to remember where we came from."

"Who said anything about forgetting where we came from?" says Right. "This is about who I am now. That's important too."

Left sighs. "So, what, you're gonna be Thomas all the time, now?"

"I don't want to be Thomas, either." Right feels his pulse quickening. He's still not quite sure if it's supposed to do that, or if he should be worried when it does. "Thomas doesn't feel like who I am, you know? It's a name we designed to be anonymous, so that I could blend in, be just another nobody in an office of nobodies. But I don't want to be nobody, I want to be me. There's no harm in that now, right? It's not like I'm hiding my body the way I had to before."

"It was anonymous at first, sure," says Left. "But you've been using it for two years now. It is who you are to a lot of people.

Right holds himself back from saying *not to me*, knowing that way lies an argument that they could go back and forth on well into the evening without ever getting anywhere, until he's too exhausted to continue and has to let it drop out of the sheer bodily need for regular rest. Besides, he knows he's gotten everything he needs out of his brother's resistance already. It's right there, he thinks: Left never wants me to stop being the other half of him. He is too stubborn, too attached to the way things were.

So he pushes the topic forward. "I've been thinking of names, and I've decided I'm going to start calling myself Allen Cleft."

Left wrinkles his nose. "I don't like it."

"You don't have to," says Right. "It's not your name."

"How do you figure? We're still brothers," says Left. "I mean, what, do I have to start calling myself Angus Cleft or something?"

"No." Right doesn't quite shout, but he can feel the shout gestating beneath his diaphragm. "Look, you don't have to be anyone you don't want to be."

"But I want to be Left. How can I be Left if you're Allen? Left and Allen? There's no symmetry to that, it's just weird."

Almost as if hanging onto this left/right thing is weird in and of itself, thinks Right. "Well, you can do whatever you want with that. You can be Left, or you can be Thomas A. Williams all the time if you want. You can be Twiddle McBandersnatch for all I care, just let me have my own name."

"*For all you care?*" Left repeats. "Shit, you make me

sound like some desperate hanger-on. Isn't this important to you? At all?"

"Sure it is," says Right, "but so is my—" Independence? Individuality? Ability to exist separately from you, not just as a literal part of your body? "—my name. Can't more than one thing be important?"

"Maybe," says Left, "but you're clearly making decisions about which things are more important than others." Right only waves his hand in response, and this strikes both of them as a suitable compromise to end the argument on: Left having gotten the last actual word, and his brother having made a non-verbal approximation of a last word. Left feels something below his diaphragm too, now, but it is more like a rock. Not something waiting to erupt, but something trying to sink into the passenger's seat of the car, and down, through the highway, into the bedrock.

Instead of thinking about the rock, he thinks about what to make for dinner. They haven't discussed dinner today, but he assumes the plan is his to make. Right—Right for just a little longer, not Allen, not yet—tries to cook sometimes, but he is not good at it. He hasn't had as much practice as Left, and it's easier for both of them if the responsibility remains his.

After dinner, he decides, they will talk about the cottage again, the same as they do most nights. That will help reconcile things, and maybe even bring Right to reconsider his name change. Remind him of what they are to each other, the importance of their continued togetherness.

***

After breakfast the next morning, Allen resolves to work on his own version of the cottage at every possible opportunity. To remind himself of what he can do on his own.

He and Left still talk about the shared version between them, but they've long since settled onto something more or less static, and the "talks" mostly consist of Left prompting

Allen to describe the same rooms he has described hundreds of times before, usually in the exact same words. For Left, the exercise seems to be about perfecting a single, finished idea, with the goal of never having to revise it again. The constant retellings are psychic reinforcement, a magic spell repeated infinitely to prevent any unwanted alterations from leaking in. When they talk, Allen imagines him pacing from room to room, painting glyphs on the walls in animal blood, going outside and sprinkling a circle of salt around the building. Even though, in reality, Left is doing nothing but talk about an imaginary house, there is something vaguely sinister about his manner that solidifies this vision for Allen.

Not only does Allen still have a separate, private version of the cottage for himself, but at this point it has lost most of its similarities to what he thinks of as the "canon version." For him, the process is more about self-discovery, a principle before which very little is sacred. His cottage has morphed and re-mixed itself, rooms have disappeared, been added back, transformed, disposed of again. Recently he has found, for the first time, that its overall size is gradually shrinking, rather than growing.

And the size isn't the biggest change he's made. His cottage is no longer in the woods; it's in a skyscraper, like one of those they see during their work commute down the outer-belt. Neither of them has ever been inside a skyscraper, but there's no reason for that to limit Allen's imagination. Inside the skyscraper, the cottage has no need of a guest bedroom, or stone hearth, or second floor. Guests can stay on the sleeper sofa, if they have any. It may be only four rooms (and a walk-in closet), but in the middle of the city they can find whatever else they need close at hand.

He supposes it would be more correct to call this arrangement an "apartment," but he still prefers to think of it as a cottage. "Cottage" is a word with a comfortable, matronly feel to it. It doesn't contain the word "apart."

Besides, even though the space is smaller, he imagines it

feeling much bigger. The cottage would be on a high floor, like the 26th. He would be able to look out the window and say, who needs a stone hearth? Who needs a big kitchen, or a veranda, or a guest bedroom? Look at everything out there! There's nothing "apart" about any of this.

The only thing that unsettles him is when he looks into the bedroom. There is only one bed, now. Where, he wonders, will Left sleep?

***

The next morning, Left is already up and dressed by the time Allen wakes up. At first, Allen worries that he overslept, and might make them late for work, but then their 5:30 a.m. alarm goes off and he knows that's not the case. He imagines Left must be full of nervous energy, after the tension between them yesterday afternoon. They talked little throughout the evening, aside from a short and halfhearted recitation of cottage schematics that only seemed to push both of them deeper into a funk.

Left doesn't seem to be in a funk now, though; it's more that he seems to vacillate between excitement and fear as he ricochets around the kitchenette, flipping eggs with jerky motions, tugging at his belt like a tic, setting coffee mugs down on the counter with more force than necessary so that they make harsh, ceramic striking sounds.

Allen shuffles out of bed, weighted by a sense of dread that today's interactions are not going to be any more comforting than last night's. When he makes it to the kitchenette, he finds his brother humming while eating his breakfast, swaying back and forth gently in the shoulders.

"Your toast is getting cold," says Left.

Allen sits down and finds that his toast is well past getting cold. "You're up early," he says.

"I lay awake all night trying to think of a new name," says Left. "I haven't slept at all, but I'm not tired. Isn't that weird?"

Allen nods drowsily. Left's mental state is familiar to him;

it's what followed a few of his most contentious nighttime conversations with Lincoln. His brother may not feel tired now, but he will soon. The only thing keeping him moving is the leftover tension from what he's been going through. "Did you pick one?" he says, bracing himself for whatever is coming next.

"I finally did!" Left smiles. "You ready? I'm going to call myself Lincoln Wright."

Allen takes a sharp breath in, bringing a few crumbs of damp, cold toast into his lungs with it. "Wright."

"With a W," Left clarifies.

Allen looks around the room, through the doorways, for any sign of the real Lincoln, the imaginary one. How can someone be both imaginary and real, he wonders in some peripheral part of his consciousness? Does this make Left not real, somehow? He finds no sign of the imaginary twin and turns to face his brother again. "I see."

Left's smile flattens. "Well, don't throw a party for me or anything."

"What do you want me to say?" Allen manages, his voice tiptoeing out between the clenching in his torso.

"I don't know, that you like it?" says Left. "That it's a good choice?"

"Ah." Allen shivers. "Yeah, it's good. It's fine."

Left shrugs. "Thanks, I guess."

The drive to work is silent. Allen finds himself wondering if he may have had a confusing dream, causing him to think that Left was his brother and Lincoln was some kind of imaginary friend. He insists to himself that he's still groggy from a restless night's sleep, and once he's fully awake, he'll remember that it was always, in fact, the opposite. That everything is fine, just as both of them have always desired.

But no matter how many trips he makes to the coffee machine between calls, the realization refuses to come. All he gets from the coffee is jitters. By mid-day, in the home stretch before their scheduled lunch break, he has reached a state of mania. He wonders if this is all happening because of the cottage: because of the mental effort of maintaining two entirely separate versions of an imaginary building, he has reached a point at which his imagination is too good, so vivid in its fantasies that he can no longer tell them from reality. How else could his real brother have the same name as his imaginary one? This, added to the fact that he hasn't actually seen this alleged imaginary brother all day, surely means that it must all be happening in his head.

1:30 p.m. arrives, and Allen makes his way to the cafeteria with his hands in his pockets, chin pointed toward his solar plexus. There must be a more practical explanation, he thinks. Nothing supernatural is going on here, and he isn't getting sucked into his own imagination or whatever he was thinking an hour ago. He must have mentioned Lincoln to Left at some point and forgotten about it. He knows he never told his brother about Lincoln, but it's possible he could have mentioned the name off-hand a time or two, just a casual remark in some unrelated conversation. But then, doesn't that mean Left must be doing this on purpose? That he held onto that name, sensing it was important, and is throwing it back at Allen now, to try to force him to accept that they can never be their own, separate people?

When it's nearly 2 o'clock, he interrupts his brooding long enough to finally notice that Left isn't with him. Normally they eat lunch together, but he's nowhere to be seen in the cafeteria now.

Allen stalks back toward his cubicle in search of his brother, who he refuses to think of as Lincoln. Using that name would be too much of an insult. He can't do it, at least, not yet. Maybe not ever. Why should he have to? It's clearly a bid for some kind of dominance. Even if the name itself is a coincidence, why would he pick "Wright" as the last name, if not to show Allen that he thinks he can control both "sides?"

As it turns out, Left is asleep at his desk. And this is the moment the real, imaginary Lincoln chooses to interpose himself.

"It's never going to be easier than it is right now," says the imaginary twin.

"What are you talking about?" Allen whispers, ducking into his own cubicle.

Imaginary Lincoln seats himself on a filing cabinet. The cubicles are so narrow, it's the only available surface not occupied by the computer. "Look, I know I'm always acting like I have all the answers, like I always know exactly what you're thinking and exactly what's going on. In my defense, that's because I'm usually right. But this? I have no idea. Don't know how he found out my name, don't know why he's decided it's his now. What I do know, though? Is that it's very, very bad. There is shit going on here that you *do not* want to get mixed up in, both in terms of emotional stuff, and . . . " He waves his hand in the air, indicating something neither of them can quite name.

"It's probably just a coincidence," says Allen.

"*Probably?*" Imaginary Lincoln snorts. "Do you know what the probability is of a coincidence like that?"

"No," Allen admits.

"Of course not, because it's one-in-a-number-so-high-we-don't-have-a-word-for-it."

"So, what, you're saying my brother is using sorcery to steal your identity?"

Imaginary Lincoln leans down, uncomfortably close to Allen's face. "Look at me, man. I'm half a guy. The reason I'm like this is because it's what you used to look like, more or less. And the only thing more incredible than the fact that you used to live, breathe, work, and eat with half a body yourself is the fact that you grew the entire other half of the damn thing like a giant fingernail. That, and the fact that you seem to have forgotten how deeply weird all of this is."

"I see what you're getting at," says Allen, "but it's not—"

"Why didn't you take him to the hospital when he was

practically in a coma because of that leg?" says Imaginary Lincoln. "Why haven't you ever tried to figure out who lived in the body that both of you came from? Hell, why do you need me around to be a sounding board for all this stuff? I'll tell you why: because you know none of this is normal. You can't rationalize it, you can't talk about it with anyone. You're alone in a world that will never make sense, with logic out the window and only your gut to rely on. So, this is your gut, telling you to get the fuck out of this situation while you've got the chance."

Allen sighs. "What are you suggesting?"

"Get your jacket, walk out of the building, drive away and keep going."

"Going where?" says Allen. "Home?"

Imaginary Lincoln shakes his head. "Go to the bank, get your money, grab anything you need from the motel room, then pick a direction and go. You can find another motel, in another town, where you're safer."

"This is nuts." Allen props his elbows on his knees and cups his forehead in his hands between them. "You're asking me to abandon my own brother."

"You can't abandon someone who doesn't want to go with you," says Imaginary Lincoln. "Your brother doesn't want to go with you. He wants you to stay with him. He wants you to abandon everything else."

"But I don't . . . really . . . have anything else?" says Allen.

"That's the point!" Imaginary Lincoln all but shakes him by the collar with his single hand. "You don't look like this anymore. You don't need to hide. You could go to any old doctor on Earth and you'd look like a completely normal middle-aged man to them. You could move to a new city, go to school, get a better job, travel. So why is this," he nods toward Left's cubicle, "*still* all you have?"

Allen considers his answer for several minutes. His lunch break is nearly over. "I still don't get what this has to do with your name."

"I told you, I don't either!" says Imaginary Lincoln. "All I know is the feeling it gives off, and what that's telling me is that, whatever is going on behind the scenes with this name thing, it doesn't lead anywhere you want to go."

"I can't just drive out of here based on a feeling," says Allen.

"Why not?" Imaginary Lincoln leans back, takes a deep breath. "Listen, it's not like you have to cut him off or anything. Even if you don't want to make any major decisions, you have to admit you could use some time to yourself right now."

"Hmm," says Allen. "I've never exactly had much time to myself."

"Well, trust me, the best time to take some is when things are tense and weird, like they are now," says Imaginary Lincoln. "Go for a drive, get some distance, text your brother when you get to wherever you're staying if you want to. Figure it out, let all the bad stuff dissipate, and then get on with your lives."

"It'll freak him out," says Allen.

"Of course it will," says Imaginary Lincoln. "You're freaked out *now*. You take care of *your* freakout, he'll take care of his. It'll be fine."

There is a long pause. "I can go back anytime, right?" says Allen.

"Whenever you want," says Imaginary Lincoln. "You can still get in touch with each other in the meantime. It's just for now."

"Yeah." Allen nods. "Yeah. I can go back whenever I'm ready."

"Whenever you're ready," Imaginary Lincoln assures him.

interlude

"Catalog" means a list, a register, a reckoning

WALKING ON EGGSHELLS is even harder with only one foot, but it can be done, especially when it must. That's another great thing about being imaginary: without the weight of a body dragging you down, there's no need to bother treading lightly. All of your weight is emotional, and it may be a lot, but at least it's all in one place.

Pity your friend, burdened with that pesky physical body. He can be seen. He can be hurt. Not you, though. You float above it all, always a witness, sometimes a commentator, but never a participant in the ugly reality of taking up space in a world where everyone seems to be fighting to take that space from you. Even when your friend yells at you, you don't feel his harsh words vibrating in your bones. Instead, you archive them, add them into the mental rubric you use to assess what you see. His pain can't hurt you, no matter how much transference he tries to affect. All it does is tell you who you're supposed to be.

If you were to look at your archive, most entries would be short and boring, notable only for the fact that there are so many of them. You can flip through them like a card catalog:

132—Parapsychology—Mental Derangement
- Brothers paranoid the metaphysical concept of death is searching for them

- Left convinced Right is not his real brother
- Right convinced he is not Left's real brother
- Left convinced he will never be "good enough" (object unknown)

134—Parapsychology—Mesmerism and Clairvoyance

- Right convinced he will never be "good enough" (due to fight with Left)
- Right eats dinner prepared by Left even though he is not hungry (due to fight with Left)
- Right does not assert his own autonomy (general /miscellaneous, due to fight with Left)
- Right does not discuss his interest in wood carving (due to fight with Left)
- Right avoids ever using the phrase "egg noodles" (due to fight with Left)
- Left convinces himself Right is going to abandon him if he doesn't exercise tight control over their relationship
- Brothers argue over layout of fictional cottage

157—Psychology—Emotions

- Left upset upon seeing Right reading a book he's unfamiliar with
- Left frightened Right might leave (due to botched dinner prep)
- Left frightened Right might leave (due to broken shower in motel room)
- Left frightened Right might leave (due to interpersonal conflict)
- Left frightened Right might leave (due to fatigue caring for disabled brother)
- Left frightened Right might leave (general/miscellaneous)
- Left upset (general/miscellaneous/reason unknown)
- Right disappointed by Left's refusal to let him collaborate on the household budget
- Right upset (work-related)

- Right upset by general ennui
- Mutual panic attack devolves into accusatory screaming match (due to car trouble)
- Mutual panic attack devolves into accusatory screaming match (due to budget shortfall)
- Mutual panic attack devolves into accusatory screaming match (due to stain on carpet)
- Mutual malaise (due to interpersonal conflict)
- Mutual malaise (due to lack of anything else to feel)

159—Psychology—Will
- Free will, lack of (due to physical disability)
- Free will, lack of (due to fear of the unknown)
- Free will, lack of (due to brother's demands)
- Free will, lack of (self-imposed)

217—Philosophy & Theory of Religion—Prayer
- Right creates imaginary friend to serve as spiritual advisor
- Left begs Right not to abandon him (unprompted)
- Left begs Right not to abandon him (due to interpersonal conflict)
- Left begs Right not to abandon him (general /miscellaneous)
- Right discusses leaving shared motel room with imaginary friend

312—Statistics—Population
- Right's belief that the world population is 7.5 billion
- Left's insistence that the world population is 2
- Right's belief that the world population is 2

397—Customs, Etiquette & Folklore—Outcast Studies
- Right looks in the mirror
- Right observes his brother

619—Medicine & Health—Experimental Medicine

- Right wonders how he was created
- Left insists that how they were created doesn't matter

This is important work, even if very little of it would be of any interest to an outside observer. It must be the focus of your life, because, when the interesting experiences do happen, you need to be there to open the drawers and show off your painstaking collection of incidents and patterns. Without your work, your friend would be stuck in them forever.

It's not that he can't figure things out on his own. He wouldn't need this from you, if it weren't for the *other* you. The one you're sure exists.

Somewhere, unseen to you, on the other side of his consciousness, is another archivist. But, instead of cataloging things that have happened, the way you do, he collects hypotheticals from all tenses: things that might happen, might have happened, might be happening now. Where you exist to clarify, he exists to sow doubt.

Here's one: 151—Psychology—Intellect—Left claims Right is not smart enough to manage finances. In this incident, Right demanded clarification for why he couldn't collaborate on the household budget (see "Right disappointed by Left's refusal to let him collaborate on the household budget").

Left responded, "Because you can't. The left brain is the analytical half, everybody knows that. Numbers and logic are my purview, the way creativity and language are yours. I do this, you do other things."

"That's not even true," said Right. "I looked into it."

"And found out what?" said Left.

"That it's a myth."

"Not a very convincing argument," said Left.

"How are you going to stop me from managing the money *I earned*?" said Right.

Left shook his head in a manner that he clearly intended

to come across as world-weary and wise. "We should all be so lucky. I can't make money like you can, and I may not even be able to once I've got a right hand. Let alone this useless leg. I mean, you can't imagine what it's like hobbling around on this thing all—"

"The leg again," Right groaned.

Left's voice rose so sharply that it startled him. "What the hell do you know about it?"

"This has nothing to do with your leg!" said Right. "I mean, shit, what *don't* I know about it? You complain about it non-stop! And don't think I haven't noticed that whenever you want to shut me up it's all *my leg this, my leg that.* You think it's easy balancing on a lopsided torso to walk around? I'm not exactly—"

Left waved his hand as if dismissing the words. "Oh, right, I forgot, being a little bit top heavy is *exactly the same* as dragging around an entire limb that you can't even use."

"And what I really think we're forgetting here—"

"Why don't you just admit that you don't care what happens to me? You just want to keep me here like a caged animal while you go out and live your life like a normal person."

Right had intended to end his sentence with *is that this has nothing to do with the household budget*, but Left's interruption paid off. He rose to the bait. "You think *I* treat *you* like a caged animal?"

The argument went on quite a while longer, especially if you're willing to count the days' worth of sulking that followed. But this is the important part. This is why you, the imaginary twin, have to keep the card catalog that he can't bear to hold onto by himself. Somewhere, your shadow self was feeding him the rationalizations, however he catalogs them. It's understandable for Left to be upset, with his leg causing him so much trouble all the time. He would be less upset if you'd phrased what you had to say differently, so what really needs to happen is that you need to pay more attention to phrasing. You shouldn't have pushed back so hard, that just alienated him more. It's no big deal, it's just one thing he wants to claim as exclusively his. Most people hate managing their finances, why aren't you glad you don't have to? It was wrong to throw his complaints about his leg back in his face, even though they *are* constant, and he *does* bring it up in situations that have nothing to do with it, and he *does* use it to minimize everything you go through, still, you should be the bigger man about it, even though you are literally just the other half of the same man, even though it *is* inconceivable to try to think of yourself as separate from him, and don't you owe him this? Shouldn't you just be nice to your brother? Shouldn't you just want to keep things civil no matter what?

If you want the mind that houses you to survive, you need to have an arsenal just as big. You need to spend every moment you have alone with him hammering on the point that the rationalizations would only work if these were isolated incidents. They're not. They're patterns. Not only that, they're patterns that grow more pronounced over time. If you can just get him to look at it all together, he'll have to see that the goal of every fight is to make asserting yourself too troublesome to go through with.

To make you walk on eggshells.

And the thing about walking on eggshells, no matter how hard it is at first, even if you're doing it one-legged? It's that if someone can get you to do it all the time for long enough, you start to just call it *walking*. You forget the eggshells are there, because they're always there. You start to think it's just the way you move through the world, the way everyone moves through the world. If anything, what you think you need is to train yourself out of resenting it.

What Right needs to see is that no matter how careful he is, there will always be another argument, because that's how humans work. If his strategy for getting through the day is to avoid any argument lest they dissolve into a fight that lasts for days, he'll always lose. The only thing that will ever change is that he'll shrink more and more into the niche Left has carved for them both.

That's the challenge: you want things to change. Left wants them not to. What does Right want? Does he know? Is that the reason you exist? To instruct him on these questions, with the end goal being that your own existence is no longer necessary? And if you succeed, what happens then?

CHAPTER 4

"Cleave" means "to cling"
and also "to divide by force"

LINCOLN CURSES HIS luck for sleeping through lunch. When he wakes and sees the time, he sneaks a quick trip to the cafeteria to get his food out of the fridge to eat at his desk. He's theoretically not supposed to do this, but the boss never says anything when he does. He notices that Right is not in his cubicle, and figures he must be in the bathroom.

After work, though, Right fails to appear. Their car is gone from the parking lot. Lincoln calls Right and follows up his voicemail with a series of texts, but there is no timely answer to either. By the time he gives up on that option, everyone else from his shift has already gone home. The office is full of people from the night shift who don't know him and who he can't ask for a ride. He has to call a cab. There goes our next bottle of scotch, he laments from the back seat.

Right isn't at home either, derailing Lincoln's plan to properly chew him out. All of his things are in their proper place, minus a few outfits and his phone charger, so Lincoln writes off the absence as part of whatever freakout made Right leave work early. His brother is going to have a lot to answer for when he gets home.

Lincoln makes dinner. A simple spaghetti and marinara, nothing he has to devote much attention to. He doesn't mind taking it easy on cooking, and if Right wanted anything better, then he should have behaved himself. Lincoln fires off a few more texts, but has no more luck than he did at the office.

By the time he goes to bed, there is still a full plate of spaghetti on the table. It remains, untouched, the next morning.

Lincoln spends one more call-and-text-filled day refusing to believe what he has suspected, in the pit of his stomach, since getting off work the previous evening. After that it's Monday—the beginning of his weekend—and he doesn't have work to distract him from the mounting fear.

He looks at their checking account and finds that a large withdrawal was made two days ago, while he was still at work. His brother took out $1,317.24. Adding the account's current balance to what he has spent on cab fare since the withdrawal, that means Right left him $1,317.23.

"Asshole," he whispers, staring at his phone's calculator app. It's the first time he's used anything close to this language for Right.

The nearest liquor store is over a mile away, but Lincoln walks there for scotch anyway.

By the time he returns to work on Wednesday, it is clear that he's going to need to come up with another car, somehow. On his break, he sits down with his calculator app and a scratch pad, planning out scenario after scenario, all with the inevitable conclusion that he'll never be able to buy himself a car if he keeps taking cabs to and from work.

The laptop in the motel room still has all the bookmarks he saved two years ago, when he first helped Right figure out how to get to the call center on the bus. It takes almost two hours each way. Strange, he thinks, that Right never complained about this.

"You used to care about me," he says to the empty bed next to his. He doesn't even have a picture of Right to say this to. Why did they never take any pictures of each other? "It was nice of you not to complain about the bus ride. I thought it was funny, how happy you were about getting the car, but I didn't understand back then."

The bed doesn't answer.

"I'm sorry."

Still nothing.

It's a week before anyone at work asks about Right. Lincoln had given HR an excuse about an illness on Right's behalf, and forged a doctor's note on stationary he printed off in the motel lobby, but the no call, noshows start piling up. Soon, Lincoln finds himself consciously ignoring emails asking how his brother can possibly still be sick.

"Where's other Thomas?" asks a coworker who started working there shortly before Lincoln did.

"He's sic—I don't know," he says.

"Damn, I hope he's all right," she says. "I would've said something sooner, but I didn't want to get nosy."

"Nosy," he repeats.

"Yeah, you know, I don't want to go poking into other people's business if they don't want me to," she explains, as if Lincoln did not know what being nosy is.

"Hmm," he says.

"You good?" she asks. "You let me know if you need anything, okay?"

"Anything," he repeats. "Sure. Thanks." He wonders how many of his coworkers have even noticed that there are two Thomases working here who are also brothers, and how many think there has only ever been one of them. With the call center's high employee turnover, there will soon be nobody remaining who remembers Right.

***

Lincoln goes to the police to file a missing persons report. He sits across a desk from a tired-looking officer who takes down his name and address, everything he knows about his brother, the circumstances when he was last seen.

"We had just had a fight . . . I think?" says Lincoln. "And he talked about wanting to change his name." He scratches at the wiry stubble on his temples, digging fingernails deep enough in his scalp to tear up little bits of skin. "Why didn't I push back more when he talked about it? I should have settled the issue then. We are who we are. If he knew that, he wouldn't have left."

The officer nods, taps a keyboard. "I'll file this," she tells him after the questions, "but it sounds like your brother is probably fine. He just doesn't want to be around you, which is pretty normal."

Lincoln frowns. "It's normal for people not to want to be around their brothers? Or do you mean me specifically?"

"I'm sure this isn't what you wanted to hear, but it is what it is," she says. "Nothing we can do about it, if that's the case. Except . . . what's this?" She squints at her computer screen. "You said your name was Lincoln Wright?"

"That's correct," says Lincoln.

"I see. Well, it says here that you're supposed to be dead."

The world dulls a few shades toward monochrome. "I . . . "

"Right here," she pokes something on the screen that Lincoln can't see, "it says you're supposed to be a cadaver at that med school down on the south side. Donated your body to science. According to my system, you're supposed to be chilling in their morgue right now."

Lincoln's voice trembles. "There must be some mistake."

"Oh! Hey, what do you know, you're right," she says. "You're not supposed to be there now. You were supposed to be there three years ago. You should've been cremated long ago. Don't worry, we'll get that all straightened out."

Every door in the precinct slams shut. Flames erupt from the desk.

"Just hop right up on there, if you don't mind," says the officer, now wearing a white lab coat.

Lincoln wakes up.

He never files a missing persons report.

He opens the cabinet and finds Right's bloated, necrosed body inside.
Roaches crawl in and out of the corpse's mouth...

*****

It takes months, but he does scrape together enough for another car. It's over twenty years old. The air conditioner doesn't work, and the engine is loud enough that there's no point asking what kind of stereo it has. In this sense, it's much like the car he shared with Right. If there are other kinds of cars that exist, it has yet to be proven to Lincoln.

Once all the paperwork is signed, he climbs in, sets his hands at ten and two, and turns the ignition. "I'm the driver now," he says. He turns to the empty passenger seat. "Why was I never the driver before? I could have done it. But it always had to be you. Why?"

The passenger seat does not respond.

Part of what made affording the car take so long is all the money Lincoln has been spending on fast food and alcohol. Still, instead of driving directly home, he goes to get fried chicken, and then to a donut shop on the other side of town.

"Gas money," he mumbles, driving home at last. "Food money. All my money now. It was better when we shared. No one to share with now, though. No point trying to save. So there."

He parks in the motel lot and starts up the stairs to their—his—room, twirling the keyring with its new addition around his thumb. He opens the door and inhales the scent of the room, the dry motel must of ashtrays and harsh cleaning chemicals. It's not a beautiful place, but it always did for him and his brother. It could have been all they needed for as long as they lived, if it had to.

When he's halfway across the room, a bolt of pain shoots up his right leg, the one that grew in too fast. He twists and drops onto the bed. "Oh, for fuck's sake," he says. "I've barely been on my feet at all."

But the pain persists all evening. He has to order pizza delivered for dinner because he can't stand long enough to cook. After hanging up the phone, he scoots across his bed, then his brother's bed, and stumbles into the chair outside the bedroom door, so he can have as few steps to travel as possible when the pizza arrives.

By the time he hears a knock at the door, something else has begun to creep underneath the smell of the motel room. Lincoln can't quite put a name to it, but it's something less artificial than its normal mustiness, a nameless, unsettling odor. Organic. Something like roast beef, but not that. Not appetizing. Familiar, but he can't say from where, except that it makes his insides feel like they're shrinking away from his skin.

He pays for the pizza and fills his nostrils with its scent instead. When he goes to bed, he sets the box with one remaining slice on the nightstand, then scoots his pillow as close to it as possible and lays down facing it. When he wakes up for work, both smells have dissipated.

He spends the first half-hour after waking gnawing on the remaining pizza slice in small, ponderous bites, staring out the window that looks onto the parking lot. After the months of long bus commutes, Lincoln barely knows what to do with all the free time he has before and after work. He sleeps longer, but there are just so many long hours of deafening solitude, and they always seem to be getting longer.

He stops driving directly home after work. Why should he have to? There's nothing waiting there except canned pasta and microwave burritos and dirty laundry. So he drives to parks, bars, movie theaters. Once he goes to a pet shop, considering a new companion, but the dogs and cats are more expensive than he anticipated. He visits the rabbits and birds, but they all seem desperate to be as far away from him as possible, crowding into the corners of their cages at his approach.

He tries hiking, and enjoys it for the first few minutes. After that, he has to limp back to the car. His bad leg is giving him fewer steps than ever before it starts complaining.

On days off, he starts driving out of town. The trips are

for a few hours at first, but he soon graduates to overnights. He prefers rural areas, which are more honest in their loneliness than the cities or suburbs. Cities especially pretend to be so full of life, but the more Lincoln sees of them, the more he understands that all they contain is very large numbers of isolated people. Even the couples he sees out and about look so *separate.* When he eavesdrops on their conversations, he is sure that they don't understand each other any better than strangers. They are so invested in the promise of intimacy, but none of them will ever truly share a body or mind with anyone else. Not the way he has.

Trees and farms, on the other hand, never feign any interest in him. He buys a tent and a sleeping bag. In the woods, it's much easier to devote his full attention to the one person capable of meeting his needs: himself. He'd prefer that this wasn't the case, but Right has never once answered a text, and now his number is disconnected.

He supposes he could devote this time to himself at the motel, but lately it unsettles him to be there. The meaty smell keeps creeping back in, no matter how much cleaning he does. One of the neighbors must be making hamburgers on the stove constantly and not cleaning up after. Well, fair's fair, he thinks, and starts leaving the sink piled with his own dirty dishes, only washing what he needs right away. It doesn't make the room smell any better, but at least now the stink is his. Besides, he only really goes there for sleep and the occasional meal.

***

Lincoln is awakened by a roach crawling across his face. He jumps from the bed as quickly as the bug jumps from him, as if neither of them expected to encounter a living creature here.

After he washes his face in the bathroom, he spots more of them exploring the dishes in the kitchenette sink, squeezing themselves through the door of the cabinet underneath. The smell makes him gag now, almost to the point of fainting.

He opens the cabinet and finds Right's bloated, necrosed body inside. Roaches crawl in and out of the corpse's mouth.

Lincoln wakes up.

He calls in sick to work and packs an overnight bag.

He doesn't check the cabinet before leaving. He can't remember whether it was Right's body he saw in the dream, or his own.

***

He picks a direction and drives until morning, on a path that guides him into the foothills. Shortly after he leaves the highway, the streetlights vanish, and it's all he can do to keep the headlights pointed at the road, which provides no hints to where it leads. The roads turn to gravel. When the soft light of dawn resolves the dark masses of trees into focus, he finds that he has somehow made his way onto a private drive. It ends a short distance ahead, in front of an old cabin with split timber walls.

There are other cars parked outside, but upon inspection they are mostly stripped-down chassis, all but one of them sitting on cinderblocks with the wheels removed. There are no power lines to be seen. Kerosene lamps sit in several of the house's windows, their glass chimneys nearly opaque with dust. A patch of shingles has come off the roof, and lies in a scattered pile by the door.

Seeing the place, Lincoln can't help but be reminded of the cottage he and Right used to talk about. In fact, the more he paces its perimeter, gauging the structure, looking into the windows to see a kitchen floor covered with red tile, a massive stone hearth in the living room, the stronger the association becomes. Lincoln isn't entirely sure whether this cabin would count as a cottage or not; nevertheless, its resemblance to the fictional house that they explored in their minds a thousand times is uncanny. There's an insistent feeling behind it, similar to the one that came to him the night he sat awake, brainstorming his new name. Yes, he is sure: this is *the* cottage, in the same way that Lincoln Wright is *the* name.

"You were here this whole time?" he asks.

The cottage does not respond.

Lincoln approaches the weathered front door. "We were supposed to get here together. What went wrong? Why did he abandon me?" He opens the door, and shuts it immediately. This place, like the motel room, has an odor. He could almost convince himself that it's the same odor, but only because of how strong it is. Something this pungent would repulse anyone. Animals have probably been living and defecating inside for years. He goes back to the car, takes a t-shirt from his overnight bag, ties it over his face, and enters the cottage, hoping to find a broom inside. He does, and gets to work with it.

The days pass. Lincoln cleans the first floor, then the second. In the guest bedroom is a wall that appears to have had holes in it patched with pieces of old furniture: a chair seat here, the front of a dresser drawer there. He finds the remaining pieces in a pile out back. The top of the pile is warped by the rain, and the bottom is half-decomposed and half-eaten by insects, but much of the rest is usable for further repairs. Soon, there are no signs that anyone but Lincoln has lived in the cottage.

He doesn't get hungry, exactly. Going days or weeks without food makes him uncomfortable, but it's more a feeling in his chest, the anxiety of knowing he's not doing something that living creatures supposedly have to do. If he doesn't eat for long enough, the stink comes back. He knows it's probably an illusion, brought on by malnourishment, but this doesn't make it any more bearable. The nearest grocery store is a half-hour drive, and he avoids it as much as possible. Civilization reminds him of his own abandonment. Once, as he is putting off another trip, he wanders into the yard, scoops a handful of humus off the forest floor, lifts it to his mouth, chews, and swallows.

There's plenty of nutrients in soil, he thinks, and it doesn't taste half bad. The flavor is sweet, a bit metallic, and even a little greasy, just enough to go down smooth. On the ground, between his knees, an earthworm pokes into the dirt crater where he scooped up his last handful. His mouth waters at the sight of it, but then he realizes what he's doing and goes back inside.

Corpses and accusations haunt his nightmares. They are his most stalwart companions. At least they never leave him.

He stops calling in sick to work when his phone runs out of battery. He doesn't return to the motel. The days grow short and blend together.

interlude

"Application" means "attaching oneself
to something new"

THINGS ALLEN NEEDS to get an apartment that he did not need to get a motel room:

- A checking account.
- A bank statement.
- A government-issued photo ID.
- A social security number.
- *Three months'* worth of rent money, for the first and last month's rent and security deposit.
- The ability to prove that he already has a job.
- The willingness to prove who he is to someone who has never met him before.
- Enough self-assured confidence to believe that he has nothing to hide. This is the piece of the puzzle that pushes him back to the motel life, at first. It takes him the better part of a week to look in the mirror and remember that he no longer has to pretend to have an entire body. Another week to remember that nobody in the real world is going to be trying to prove that he doesn't; those are just bad dreams, however frequent they may be.
- A new library card, having left his with Left at the old motel. He needs the computers there to get and organize the other things he needs.

- A new e-mail address, so that he can get another library card.
- A new phone, having thrown his off a bridge when he realized he'd rather do that than keep getting messages from Left.
- Research into the process of getting a social security card. There is a government office downtown where he can do this, but he can't start the process until he's sure he'll have an answer to every question they're going to ask.
- A place for the car to stay parked while it's broken down.
- Bus fare to get to the social security office downtown, and everywhere else he needs to go.
- Getting an apartment, he comes to learn, is probably the most complicated thing he has ever done. At the same time, it's something millions of other people seem to go through with minimal complaint. So there has to be a way.
- A way to silence the voice in his head that tells him all his efforts are doomed to failure before they begin. Sometimes the voice sounds like his real brother, and sometimes it sounds like his imaginary friend. It is hard to tell the difference, because they sound very similar, and both of them now claim to have the same name. He would be hard pressed even to say what the difference is between them, but somehow he is always able to figure it out. It's the minutiae of the voices that is subtly different; only someone who is used to navigating the moods of both people would be able to tell.
- A job.
- References, for the job application. He supposes he could look for a job that doesn't ask for references, but all the pet stores and animal shelters in town require them.
- Courage, to write in his references as people from the call center, taking it on faith that they won't reveal to Left where he's gone.

- A bottle of cheap whiskey, his companion for a night spent in the back of the broken-down car contemplating the lengths to which he has gone to avoid any contact from his brother.
- A bottle of pain relievers.
- A list of common job interview questions that he can use to prepare.
- A blank check for his direct deposit form.
- A current address to put on the job application and the rental application. This is what pushes him back into a motel for the second time.
- Enough forward emotional momentum not to think about what will happen if he runs out of money he can use for the motel room before he gets the job or the apartment.
- The ability to compartmentalize everything that he has done, and everything that has happened to him, with the promise to himself that he'll deal with it later, after the immediate concerns of housing, food, and employment are taken care of. He can feel the ghosts of these events floating over his shoulder, just out of view, at every moment of the day. He can hear them in the back of his skull, smell them trying to putrefy and bloom into the miasma of despair that he's holding back with every ounce of will he's got. There are moments when it feels like he could touch them, if he tried. Like he could reach over his shoulder and find the warm, fleshy mass of his doubts waiting to look him in the eye, to fuse itself to him irrevocably, to make him serve them. There are moments when it feels like he *wants to* serve them. It wouldn't be fulfilling, or liberating, or any of the things he came here looking for. But it would be comfortable. It would be something he knows.

Things Allen does not need to get an apartment:
- A brother.
- An imaginary friend.

CHAPTER 5

"Cellar" means "a concealed place"

IT'S WINTER WHEN the neighbor comes by. Lincoln was not aware that he had a neighbor at the cottage, but here he is, knocking at the door, already aware of the broken doorbell.

"Neighbor! You're back!" says the man. He's middle-aged and energetic, with a neatly trimmed salt-and-pepper beard constituting the only hair on his head. Without any invitation from Lincoln, he enters the cottage and throws his tan Carhartt on the chair in the living room.

Lincoln decides not to question the word "back," since bringing it up might force him to admit that he is technically squatting. Given that this is the first appearance of the neighbor in several months of his being here, Lincoln thinks it's likely he doesn't visit often. Maybe rarely enough that he doesn't fully remember what the original resident looks like, and Lincoln can simply go on allowing him not to remember.

"Hi, uh, neighbor," says Lincoln. He feels a slight scrape along his palette as the words come out. It's been so long since he last spoke to another person. "Please, come in."

The neighbor spreads his arms. "Way ahead of you, buddy. Hug?"

Lincoln obliges a stiff hug, thinking of the day he left the hospital with Right, each one's arm around the other's waist.

"Just you here, huh?"

Lincoln's eyes shift around the room, looking for any as-yet-overlooked clue as to who else the man believes to live here. He tries to play it off. "You were expecting someone else?"

"Well, one can hope." The man seats himself in the green leather armchair across from the fireplace. "One can always hope. I'm guessing this is the part where I need to introduce myself. You forgot my name again, right? That's fine, I'm used to it. It's Clove, short for Clover. Not Clive. I know it's confusing. Blame my parents." From the cuff of his sleeve, he produces a piece of what appears to be tree bark, bites off half, and offers the rest to Lincoln. "You doing all right?" he asks, when Lincoln doesn't respond.

"Yes! Yeah, sorry. I was just thinking about my brother for some reason."

"Mm, you don't say." Clove stuffs the bark back up his sleeve. Whenever he's not talking, he chews the piece he bit off like gum. "How is your brother, if you don't mind my asking?"

Lincoln sits in the other living room chair, the brown leather one with Clove's coat hanging off the back. "I do, actually."

"Not on good terms, then." Clove frowns.

Lincoln offers a silent prayer that the neighbor isn't planning to stay long, despite the fact that he can see him unlacing his boots. "Sorry," he says, "I'd offer you a snack or a drink or something, but I haven't been to the store in a while." He doesn't specify that this is because his checking account is dry.

"Oh, I'm in good shape in the snack department," says Clove. "You sure you don't want some? It's birch."

"I'm fine."

Clove scratches at his beard. "Well? Fill me in, how'd it go this time? I must have been waiting ten years, this time around, or what felt like it. No need to keep me in suspense."

Lincoln turns his head toward the window, hoping to hide the flush he's taking on, courtesy of his nerves. "This time," he repeats. "Um, sorry but can you remind me what you're talking about?"

"You know, since the last time we spoke. This go-around. What happened?"

"Could you be more specific?" The words come out noticeably louder than Lincoln intended, from his attempt to project confidence over the tremor in his voice.

Clove stands, crosses the room to where Lincoln is seated, stoops down close to his face so that he can't possibly look away. He sniffs the air in front of Lincoln, spits a wad of chewed-up bark into the corner, and sniffs again. "I'm gonna ask you a question," he says, "and I want you to be real honest with the answer. I'll know if you're lying, you get me?"

Lincoln nods.

"You ever met me before?"

Lincoln manages a nervous shake of his head.

"I'll be damned."

"I . . . " Lincoln swallows. "Please don't call the cops or anything. I'm not hurting anyone by being here. This place is abandoned. I know it's not my house, but—"

"I wouldn't worry about that," says Clove. "One thing I can tell you for sure is that this is your house. Says so on the deed, this cottage belongs to Lincoln Wright. And before you put your brain in stitches trying to figure out if you ever introduced yourself since I came to the door, you didn't. I know your name, because I'm your neighbor. Although I suppose I'm not a neighbor in the traditional sense, if you take my meaning. Besides which, I don't even know what calling the cops would look like, this far off the beaten path. I think you'd get a quicker response from the Forest Service."

"Where do you live?" says Lincoln.

Clove chuckles, shakes his head, returns to his own chair. "I live close by. Don't worry about that, either. You worry about you, my friend. So really, where is your brother?"

"I don't know," Lincoln admits.

"Hmm." Clove bobs his head from side to side. "Could be worse. For a minute I was worried you'd killed him again. Mind if I smoke?" He produces a cigarette and lighter from the pocket of his work shirt, holds both near his mouth just out of view, and quickly puffs three rings of thick, white smoke that doesn't smell like tobacco. "I know, I know, filthy habit. Can't teach an old dog new tricks, though, and in dog years I am very, very old."

Lincoln sniffs at the bluish-white smoke drifting out of the cigarette. It has a wet, mossy odor that makes him think about his experiment, months ago, eating dirt. The thought produces an uncomfortable, if increasingly familiar, churning in his guts. He allows it, because it's easier to deal with this discomfort than it would be to try to grapple with every single side-comment his self-proclaimed neighbor makes. "Why do you care about my brother so much?"

"If either of us should be asking that question, it's me."

"Why do *I* care about my brother so much?" Lincoln huffs. "He's my brother."

"I happen to have a brother myself," says Clove. "Visits around the solstices. We get along okay. Don't have many deep conversations. He lives somewhere up north, and I'm never completely sure what it is that he does up there."

"It doesn't sound like you're very close."

Clove blows a stream of the peaty-smelling smoke. "We're not."

"Doesn't that make you sad?"

"No." Clove chuckles. "No, no. We're different people, it's as simple as that. Besides which, I've got plenty of other ways to amuse myself. Brothers aren't the only important thing in the world. So I'm gonna ask you again: why do you care about your brother so much?"

Lincoln avoids making eye contact. Odds are, he decides, that he's having another nightmare and Clove is about to tell him that he's supposed to be dead, or else he's going to look away and look back to find that Clove has turned into Right, just before he dissolves into a pile of maggots. He wills himself awake, but has no luck.

"We . . . " Lincoln makes a soft, guttural noise, not loud enough to hear, but enough to rattle the anxious itching in his temples. "We were in a hospital."

"Sounds pretty believable to me," says Clove. "I'd bet real money there's plenty of people in hospitals right this very minute."

"It was the morgue." Lincoln forces himself to take a breath at the end of the sentence, and transitions into the more-believable lie he has practiced. "They thought we were dead. Both of us. But we weren't."

Clove smirks, eyes focusing on the far distance. "My brother thought I was dead, once. Best practical joke I ever played, almost."

"Well, *we* didn't think it was funny." Lincoln frowns. "I bet if you woke up in a morgue, you'd be pretty freaked out too. So we booked it out of there and found a place to crash. Right got a job at a call center, and—"

"That's your brother's name? Right?"

Lincoln mutters disparagingly at himself. He should have said Thomas. "Your name is Clover," he says.

"Fair point!" Clove slaps his knee. "Fair point. Who am I to judge a good, old-fashioned human name, right? Right, Right?" he says, to an empty space next to Lincoln's chair. "People pick stranger ones, I suppose. When I was younger, my neighbors had a dog named something white folks don't like to say anymore. Not in public, anyway."

"What's in that?" says Lincoln, nostrils flaring. "Whatever you're smoking?"

"Water, mostly," says Clove. "Like you. Open a window, if you like."

Lincoln shakes his head, the mention of smoke having filled his head with images of meat hanging in a smokehouse. I'm not dead, he tells himself; I'm not meat.

Clove puts the cigarette out on the bottom of his boot,

then tucks the butt into his sleeve. "Didn't you have anyone else?"

"Anyone else what?"

"You know, friends. Lovers, god forbid. Anyone in your life besides your brother, you get me?"

"I had coworkers," says Lincoln.

"Mm-hmm," says Clove. "Who you'd see outside of work?"

"Why would I do that?"

"You wouldn't," says Clove. "You never do. It's the damnedest thing. Give most folks a chance, an actual chance to go back and try again, they probably will do things differently. Give them 100 chances, they'll do it 100 different ways. But some things don't change. Some things you'll always do the same way, because you're still yourself."

"What are you saying?" says Lincoln. "That they'll do it differently, or that they won't? It can't be both."

"It's not the outward actions that are always the same," says Clove. "It's what underlies them. Motivation, some people call it. Has to do with your assumptions about the world and its folk. In your case, the idea that you can build an entire world with just two people in it. I suspected that was the case, but now I'm really sure. I could give you all the chances in the world to make things right with your brother, Allen or Carver or Thomas or *Right*, or whatever you're calling him on any given go-around, and it wouldn't matter because you're still you. You still assume the same things."

As Clove speaks, Lincoln's brain seems to zoom out of the conversation and begin reflecting on how cold he knows it is inside the house. Keeping the poorly insulated cabin warm enough to live in has been a constant struggle as winter sets in, but for some reason he has ceased to notice the cold since the neighbor arrived. He puts a hand to his neck and finds his carotid artery throbbing like a bass drum.

"I don't understand what you're talking about," says Lincoln.

"Of course not." It feels like Clove is looking through Lincoln, not really talking to him anymore. "We've done this so many times, there's barely any of you left. You don't remember me, you don't remember all your other tries . . . you've lost everything. Stripped bare. I think the you I'm seeing now must be the truest version of yourself, torn down to the essentials. And let me tell you, those essentials are *bleak*."

"I think you should leave," says Lincoln.

Clove doesn't heed him this time. He rises from his chair and stoops over Lincoln like he's looking at an unusually large cockroach. "Most people get the picture after a few attempts: if you regret what you've done, change who you are. Cope with who you've been and decide to grow instead of repeating the same mistakes again and again. Not you, though. There's something in you that resists that growth. What is it, I wonder?" His hand drifts to the top of Lincoln's head and tilts it back until they are staring directly into each other's eyes.

Lincoln slaps the hand away. "Get. Out."

Clove smirks, leans forward and starts lacing his boots back up. He doesn't break eye contact with Lincoln. "You think me leaving'll help you?"

"Get *out!*" Lincoln rises so fast that his chair topples over backwards. "Get out! *Get out!*"

"I'll be seeing you around, then," says Clove. He stands, takes his coat, and crosses to the door in one step, seeming almost to float across the floor as he does.

Lincoln takes the kerosene lamp from the windowsill and hurls it after Clove, but the man has already left. The lamp shatters against the edge of the door frame. Lincoln doesn't clean it up, and spends the rest of the day huddled under musty blankets in the bedroom. He doesn't go outside or even look out the window. If Clove is still out there somewhere, it will prove that this isn't another horrible dream.

***

That night, it occurs to Lincoln that he hasn't eaten in a while. A very long while; in fact, he's not totally sure when the last time was that he ate anything.

In the warmer seasons, he might be able to find raspberries growing wild in the woods, or, failing that, nab a few ears of corn from a nearby farm. Being winter, his choice is between driving into town to shoplift from the grocery store, or figuring something else out.

He puts on the heavy winter coat he found in the closet, takes his basket, and goes out into the woods to scrape bark from trees. Moist, mossy tree bark. He tears it away, strip by strip, and drops it into the basket like pieces of beef jerky. What a haul, he thinks, when the basket is full.

Back at the cottage, he transfers all the bark into a stew pot, pours water from the rain barrel over it, and sets it to simmer. Preparing meals is second nature to Lincoln, and he moves through the process, barely aware of what he's doing, following a recipe in his mind that consists more of a series of abstract ideas than a set of steps and measurements. By the time the bark has begun to dissolve, the soup taking on a more uniform texture, he has stripped naked. He twists his shirt into a loaf-shaped ball, places it on the counter, and dices it finely, then does the same with his other garments.

Lincoln walks over and sniffs the soup. "Not time to add these yet," he says to nobody in particular. It's important to follow the methods he knows. Add the clothes too early and they'll be soggy by the time it's done. "Another hour, maybe."

Something about this feels off. It shouldn't take this long for the ingredients to cook. It must be the difference in altitude, messing up the timing that he's used to. Unfortunately, his appetite is just as insistent at this altitude as ever; at least, now that he's remembered an appetite is something he has.

Lincoln still hasn't explored the cottage's cellar much, so

he decides to check it for other ingredients he could add while he's waiting for the soup. Any human-produced food left down there would have surely been scavenged by animals long ago, but maybe there's a carcass lying around that he can feed off of. Something with good marrow still in the bones, maybe even a little meat.

The cellar has a dirt floor, which he has to remind himself not to eat. "Dirt isn't food," he mutters as he shuffles between shelves cluttered with tools, empty flowerpots, old magazines. He selects a rusty saw from one of the shelves. "Iron is good for you," he reassures himself, and begins licking corroded flakes off the blade. A milk crate sits overturned nearby, and he takes a seat there, cross-hatched plastic pressing into his fleshy bottom, as he snacks.

Across the room, from this vantage point, Lincoln notices a square wood panel lying on the floor. No, in the floor; the panel is recessed slightly below the dirt. He leans forward, coming to rest on his knees, and scoots closer. As the panel comes into better focus in the gloom of the basement, he can make out hinges attached to one side, a handle on the other.

He sits up on his haunches. That can't possibly lead anywhere, right? he asks himself. Rustic cottages don't have sub-basements. And yet, the longer he stares at it, waiting for its true shape to come into focus, the more his eyes adjust and confirm what it appears to be: a door, set into the dirt floor, presumably leading farther down.

Leaning forward, he reaches his hand above the door, just a few inches from its surface, and feels a light, warm breeze on his palm.

He pulls his hand away. Looks at the saw in his other hand and really tastes, for the first time, the fact that he has been licking rust off a piece of metal. Catches a whiff of the parody of soup he's been making upstairs, rank like simmering bog muck. It's like he's a child, play-acting with plastic imitations of food. He vomits onto the dirt.

"What the hell am I doing?" he groans, as the last dry heaves of his fit announce themselves. "What the fuck?"

Lincoln climbs out of the cellar, muttering the whole way. "What the fuck. What the fuck." He takes the simmering tree bark off the stove, tosses it out the back door. "What. The fuck." Sweeps his diced outfit into the trash, goes to the master bedroom and dresses himself from the overnight bag he's still living out of. He gets into bed and draws the covers over himself. He's freezing. It's the middle of winter and he's been wandering naked around a house with holes in the roof.

Shivering, stomach empty, Lincoln lies in bed and tries to make sense of the way he has spent the evening. I must be delirious from hunger, he thinks. Maybe I really am nothing without Right.

Even though his veins are tight with fear, his stomach still churning from what's been done to it, and the house still freezing from the window he left open that morning and then forgot about, he finds his body giving in to sleep.

***

Clove comes over again the next morning. Or, at least, what feels like the next morning to Lincoln, though it's impossible to tell if it's been eight hours, or if he's been huddled in the bed without the strength to get up for days or weeks that have felt like one continuous night. Clove lets himself in without knocking. Lincoln listens helplessly to the sound of the door opening and shutting, the thud and creak of each footstep in the thin-walled echo of the cottage.

"What are you gonna do to me?" he whispers when Clove enters the bedroom.

Clove doesn't appear to have heard him. "Rise and shine, Lincoln Wright, it's the weekend!" He picks up the trash can, then wrestles the bedroom window open long enough to toss its contents into the side yard. He flips the can over to use as a chair, next to the bed.

Lincoln doesn't find himself any more motivated to move by the blast of cold air from the window.

"I noticed yesterday you haven't got much to eat around here, so I figured I'd run by the bakery before coming over." Clove says this as if *the bakery* were a place that both of them should immediately recognize, despite being in the middle of the woods with no services for miles. "Want a bagel? Baker's dozen, fresh from the oven." Lincoln doesn't respond, so he continues, "The answer is yes, you do. Starving to death is a rotten way to go. Believe me, I've witnessed it. Let's see, here . . . I didn't get any of the ones with cheese or chocolate chips or any of that garbage, so I hope you're in a more traditional mood. Want a sesame seed one? Pumpernickel?"

Lincoln doesn't poke his head out from under the blanket, but he mutters, "pumpernickel," and feels a lump of dough tossed onto the bed beside him.

"Go slow," Clove coaches him. "Looks like that belly of yours has been empty for a while. Needs some time to stretch. It's like exercise, you can't just dive into the serious stuff without a warm-up. You'll give yourself cramps."

"I feel nauseous already," says Lincoln. "The food doesn't taste right."

"What's it taste like?"

"Not food."

"Might have something for that. Just a minute . . . there we go. Have a chew on this." Clove passes Lincoln a peeled root vegetable that turns out to be raw turmeric, gritty against his tongue, overwhelming his sinuses.

"This doesn't taste much better," Lincoln complains.

"Doesn't make you nauseous, though, does it?" says Clove, and Lincoln has to admit that it does seem to help. "Let that old witch's carrot digest for a bit, then try the bagel again."

Lincoln tries another bite of the bagel. His stomach objects, but not as loudly as before, so he lays back onto the pillow and lets digestion do its work.

Seizing the opportunity, Clove continues. "I'm a friend, Lincoln. I know you don't think you've known me that long, but I've been looking out for you for a good while. I'm not about to let you go hungry. And I don't just mean food, I mean in any sense of the term. You've got a whole lot of different kinds of hunger eating away at you, and we're not gonna let them get you down any more than they already have. You can count on me, neighbor."

"Last night I thought I was hungry for tree bark and rust," says Lincoln. "I think I'm going crazy."

"Crazy," Clove repeats. "There's another word some folks don't like to use anymore. Personally I don't mind it, though. Crazy is a very useful thing to be. Crazy bends the rules, changes your perspective, opens a door for things to step through that couldn't normally make it out in the real world. Things like yours truly."

"You?"

Clove chuckles. "That was a joke, neighbor, a joke. I handle the real world just fine. It's you we need to worry about. I mean, you didn't *really* want to eat that stuff, did you? But you thought you did, and I bet it was that old brain of yours trying to get some of your more eccentric hungers figured. Got to keep an eye on that brain, or it's going to start playing practical jokes on its own damn self. Hilarious ones. I mean, hilarious if you're on the right side of the equation."

Lincoln finds that the turmeric, disgusting though it was, is doing its work. The feeling in his belly is back to normal, and the bagels smell like bagels, rather than the disturbingly familiar rotten scent he initially got off them. He sits up. "Whatever happened to me last night, I never want to be that kind of hungry again."

"You may have come to the wrong place then," says Clove. "All kinds of hunger floating around out here in the woods. You never know when those unfamiliar varieties are going to come knocking."

"Where else could I go?"

Clove shrugs. "You could go back to the city. Get a job, get a place, work on yourself."

"That wouldn't help me find my brother again, though, would it?"

"See, this is what I love about you, Lincoln," says Clove, and Lincoln feels his stomach sink down into his pelvis, sensing that he's fallen into some kind of trap. "I can give you all the answers point blank, and you just keep on coming back for more. Everything is *my brother this* and *my brother that*, you stay fixated on a past that won't change no matter how many times you try to relive it."

"I've never relived my own past," Lincoln objects. "There's no such thing. You keep acting like I'm some kind of time traveler or something, but I've only lived this one life."

"How do you think you got into that morgue?" says Clove.

"I don't know!" Lincoln admits. "I don't remember anything before that, but it sure as hell wasn't by repeating the past few years over and over!"

"I love it. I love it!" Clove slaps his knee. "Just like any human, you're sure that what you can't remember must not have happened!" He rises from his chair, bends forward uncomfortably close to Lincoln's face, and touches a hand to his cheek. "We've done this to the point where you're starting each repetition as a complete blank slate with no idea how you were made or what it was done for, and still, *still* you keep repeating the same patterns! If I were an academic, I'd get myself a nice, fat grant just for keeping you around."

This time, Lincoln doesn't have the energy to be angry. He thinks about the hospital. About waking up on the table, he and his brother, seeking each other in the dim light leaking under the door. He relaxes into the memory, finds it perfectly fitted to the shape of him, so much softer and warmer than the mildewy-smelling bed he rests in. Everything about them so pure, and vulnerable, and right there.

Clove continues. "But look, you don't need to be afraid of me. I'm not trying to make a *study* of you or keep you in a zoo or anything like that. I just want to help. Be a good neighbor. Sorry if I get a little excited when I'm ruminating out loud. I believe it's that tendency of mine that's kept me single all these years. I know it comes out sounding ugly sometimes, but the difference between me and most people is that they have the same kinds of thoughts, they're just afraid to say them out loud. How's that bagel?"

"Finished," says Lincoln, grateful, at least, for a question he can easily answer.

"Well, there's more where that came from," says Clove. "Want another? How about coffee? I could make some."

"I don't have any coffee." In response, Lincoln hears the soft crinkle of a paper bag as Clove places the bagels on the bed next to his pillow.

"You will soon, then. Eat as many of those as you want, I'll be right back. Those are all for you, I don't need 'em. You need anything else, just call, okay? I'm right downstairs."

It only takes one more bagel to fill Lincoln's belly nearly to bursting. After so long not eating, there isn't much room for anything in his gut besides anxiety. He lays on his back, belly toward the sky, giving it as much space as possible to digest. Despite the discomfort, he finds himself relaxing into the role he now occupies. Here I am again, he thinks, unable to get up lest his own body overwhelm him with pain, dependent on someone else for his survival. It's a lot like when his leg grew in too fast. It wasn't a pleasant few weeks, but he looks back on that time with fondness. There was, at least, a sense of security to it. And isn't it better to be secure in pain than cast adrift into the uncertain world?

A few hours later, when he's able to rise, he goes downstairs to thank Clove for the help, but he's nowhere to be found on the ground floor. Not wanting to believe that he really left without saying anything, Lincoln decides to check the cellar. There's no more light down there during the day than there was at night, but it feels safer, somehow. The trap door is nowhere to be seen. The corner is nothing but the bare dirt floor.

His hunger returning, Lincoln plods back upstairs in pursuit of another bagel. He opens the bag and finds it in exactly the same state as the cellar floor: nothing but dirt. The pain in his gut returns. He vomits into the bag, a stream of black beetles covered in mucous, then wakes up.

He flees his bed, briefly certain that it really is full of the beetles he threw up. He goes downstairs. The pantry is stocked with canned goods and large, ceramic jars full of flour, sugar, bulk grains. The coffee maker is full of fresh brew that smells rich as pecan pie. He pours it down the sink. Days go by before he is willing to touch any of the food.

***

Clove doesn't visit for weeks. After the bagels, Lincoln finds himself wondering whether he was ever there at all. The neighbor who visits from nowhere, who tells him they've known each other for years despite Lincoln remembering nothing of the man? It seems all the more implausible, after whatever it was that happened last time. Still, Lincoln isn't sure whether the idea of Clove being real is more or less disturbing than the idea of him being purely a dream figment.

The pantry is always stocked. He resists the food at first, giving in only when he's practically starving, but it all proves to be quite real. With food no longer the concern it was, he fills his days with everything he can manage to do with loneliness. The sun rises and falls while the weather stays cold. His routine mostly revolves around huddling under blankets and flipping idly through a Bible he found in the living room with half the pages torn out, in between cooking meals and whatever housework needs to be done.

Winter stretches on and the walls of the cottage seem to grow thinner. "What good is all this lumber?" he asks the rafters one afternoon. The rafters don't respond. "I almost think I'd be better off with a tent and a sleeping bag. Houses are meant for families. With me here by myself, all this place does is crumble."

He checks the cellar several more times for the trap door, hoping, if nothing else, to lay his body on top of the warm breeze he remembers coming from it. It doesn't reappear. Once, figuring he has nothing better to do, he takes a trowel from the shelves and starts to dig where he remembers seeing it. He digs a few inches down, presses his hand to the dirt to feel its temperature, and repeats. When the hole is deep enough to reach his arm in up to the elbow, he finds that the dirt actually does feel strangely warm. He excavates a few inches more and finds solid rock, cold as a frosted windowpane.

He taps his fist on the rock, as if knocking on a door. Nothing happens, but that night he dreams that deer, and squirrels, and crows, and all manner of woodland creatures keep coming up to his bedroom window to look in at him and laugh. He suspects they are laughing at him because he knocked on the rock. Their laughter sounds human at first, but the same animals keep coming back for another look and laughing harder and harder, as if he became more outrageously funny the longer he continues to do nothing. As they fall further and further into their riotous ecstasy, they begin breaking into crow caws, squirrel titters, the high, creaky squeals of deer, groundhogs' whistling chuckles, fox screams.

He awakens, heart pounding, skin drenched with cold sweat. It's just after 3 a.m. Thinking about the nightmare, Lincoln finds that he can't remember what about it was all that scary. But he also finds that he isn't comfortable being in a room with windows.

The hole he dug in the basement floor is just the right size for a body, if he tucks his knees into his chest. The rock at the bottom even feels surprisingly soft, like a bed of moss.

Wrapped in blankets from the bed, it's the most comfortable sleep he's gotten since Right disappeared.

He wakes again in the afternoon, realizes where he is, and scrambles out of the hole. I almost buried myself, he thinks. Like a dead person.

"Am I?" he whispers. He climbs the ladder out of the cellar, goes into the bathroom, wets his sleeve and wipes away enough grime from the mirror to look himself in the face. "Dead? Am I dead? Is that why all the animals were laughing?"

Look at the dead human! He thinks he's alive! He doesn't know when to quit! He thinks a heartbeat is all it takes to fool the reaper! He doesn't know you need a soul in there too!

***

For the first time in months, Lincoln opens the door of his car and climbs inside. There is still gas in the tank, maybe enough to make it back to the city, but he can't bring himself to turn the ignition. Even if the cottage brings him nothing but cold and loneliness and hunger, even when every sigh of the settling structure is a reminder of his inability to hold onto his brother, the man who was once part of him in body and spirit, still he finds that leaving this place holds no appeal. Where would he go? He recalls Clove's taunts about getting a job and working on himself, but would that make his life any less desolate? Would it return Right to him? How can he hope to hold onto anything if he can't hold onto his own family?

He inhales deeply. Air fills lungs that feel vacant, dusty, as if he had not been breathing until it occurred to him to do so. Thinking on it, he realizes that he didn't eat a meal yesterday either, despite the cottage being consistently well stocked.

I'm forgetting how to live, he realizes. Without Right, I'm fading away. I'm part of nothing. No meaning to anyone in the whole world. Except, maybe, for Clove.

Their laughter sounds human at first, but the same animals keep coming back for another look and laughing harder and harder, as if he became more outrageously funny the longer he continues to do nothing.

He exits the car, leaving the keys inside. Striping naked, he leaves his clothes on the hood. He feels the cold, but only a little.

In the cellar, the trap door is back. He flings it open, warm air buffeting his face. The hole he dug earlier isn't there, nor is the bedrock. He's looking down into bottomless nothing.

"I've got to hand it to you," Clove says from somewhere below. "It took longer than I expected. I was starting to think you'd finally decide enough is enough, this time around. I gave you the food. Could have given you more than that. But you only really want one thing, don't you?"

"My brother."

"Some people go their whole lives without ever having a brother," Clove says thoughtfully. "You know that? A lot of them do just fine."

"Not me," says Lincoln. "I need to go back. I need another shot at getting it right. If there's even a chance it won't turn out like this again, I have to try. It doesn't matter how much food I have, if there's no one to share it with."

"And the person you share it with has to be your brother?" says Clove. "No one else?"

"Look at me," says Lincoln. "Look at what I am, where I come from. Who else could there be?"

"No one, with that attitude," says Clove. "You sure this is really what you want? You could load that old car full of canned food, drive back into town and start over for real. Really, truly make a new you, without all this baggage weighing you down."

"No," says Lincoln. "There's nothing real about that. There's only one way for me to start over for real, and that's to do it from the beginning."

"Well, all right. Suit yourself." Clove sighs audibly, and another burst of warm air brushes Lincoln's face, like an exhalation. Like it's not a door he's opened in the dirt floor, but a mouth, and the gaping maw of the Earth is the direct source of his neighbor's voice. "Why don't you come on down, then?"

Lincoln closes his eyes, offers a silent prayer to whoever might be listening, and shifts into a sitting position, dangling his legs over the edge of the trap door. It feels a bit like dipping them into a warm bath, but the darkness below is thicker than water, and clings to his skin more tenaciously. It embraces him, welcomes him, envelops him, almost seems to sing as it runs over his body. He plunges in, giving his whole self over to its care.

The darkness receives him, guides him gently onto his back, resting him on a soft, invisible table. The razor edge of something more solid presses itself to his navel. A ridge of jagged, metal, W-shaped teeth. A permanent smile, flecked with rust from all its exposure to the open air.

When Clove's voice comes to him, it's less of a sound than a rattle inside his skull, buzzing against his temples and conducting itself into his brain. "Now, I won't lie to you, this is going to hurt. It's going to hurt a lot. But, you know what they say about the pain of childbirth. Soon forgotten. You ready?"

Left thinks back to the first time he found himself on a table. Struggling into consciousness, abandoned by the world, his body cavity open and vulnerable and pulsing. He remembers reaching out across the impossible void of the universe to find his brother, his other half, waiting for him just out of sight. Standing up and seeing each other for the first time, each one a perfect reflection of the other, and knowing, without a doubt, what it would take for each of them to be complete. Holding their bodies tight against each other and saying "I love you" in a language that only they understand. Everything about them so pure, and vulnerable, and right there.

"Breathe out when it hurts the most," says Clove.

Left breathes out.

CODA

DOWNTOWN IS MOSTLY vacant after dark, which is something that Allen appreciates. He enjoys the space, the openness, the silence of the buildings that are so busy with commerce during the day, dotted with the occasional dive bar oasis that serves the second-shift workers, the lawyers and businessmen pulling late nights. After his shifts at the animal shelter, he often lingers here for hours, a library book tucked under his arm, drifting between the bars and bus stops and park benches, spots where he can sit and read or not read, play his own little part in the vastness of the world around him.

It's Sunday, which means he doesn't have work, but he finds himself on the bus into town anyway. Maybe he's craving the night air, maybe he's restless and just needs to be in motion. It doesn't especially matter, as long as the choice feels right.

"Whatcha reading?" asks the man occupying the two seats across the aisle. Allen flashes him the cover of his current book. The man nods. "Never heard of it. Any good?"

"I'm enjoying it," says Allen.

"Not much of a reader myself, but good on ya," says the man.

"Right on," says Allen, who has learned that this, strange as it seems, is just the kind of conversation people have on the bus.

The process of figuring out things like this—how to act on the bus, or in a coffee shop, or at a job where he interacts with people who actually want to be talking to him—was harsh at first, and every day in the city felt like pushing a boulder up an impossibly steep hill. Now, it's hard for him to believe that he has only been here eight months. Less than a year, and he already feels the time he spent in the motel with his brother fading into something beyond memory, more like a bad dream that he finally awakened from. They were together there for more than three years, which felt endless at the time, but also might have been three weeks, for all the emotional growth the two of them went through in that time.

Physical growth, of course, that's another story. But Allen finds himself thinking about that less and less as time goes by, too. The experience shaped him in certain ways, of that he's certain, but it had little to do with who he is, or what he wants, or almost anything that has happened since. All of that time, he was just waiting for the life he has now to come along, only to learn that he could have stepped out the door and started living it almost anytime he wanted.

The two men exchange no more words on the bus, but they get off at the same stop and find themselves walking the same direction.

"Going my way?" the stranger says cordially.

Allen gestures at the bar on the corner. "Just getting a drink."

"You too, huh?" the stranger chuckles. "Good place. Pretty generous with their shots."

"Yep."

Allen walks a respectful distance behind the other man, mostly for the sake of avoiding more awkward small talk. The stranger enters the bar ahead of him, and when Allen gets inside he and the bartender are already having an animated conversation.

The bartender nods to Allen. "This your brother?" he says to the other man.

"What, me?" says Allen. "No, no."

"Cousin then?"

"We're not related," says the other man, who holds out his hand. "I'm Allen."

A chill runs down Allen's spine. "Oh. Uh, me too." He looks at the other man, really considers him for the first time. They're not related, of course, Allen isn't related to anybody besides his estranged brother, but he can see where they could be. The man is older, probably nearing retirement age, and even with the shape of his body concealed by a baggy windbreaker and dungarees it's clear that he's a slighter build than Allen. But he does see some of himself there. Little features, mostly in his face. When he shakes the other Allen's hand, it feels almost like clasping his own two hands together.

"Well this is awkward," says the other Allen, "what am I gonna call you? No, never mind, you can just use my middle name. So, let's try that again. Hi, I'm Isaiah."

"I-sai-ah," the bartender intones. "I'd definitely be going by Isaiah if that was my middle name."

"Anyway, nice to meet you, Allen," says Isaiah. "Have one on me. Least I can do for stealing your name."

Allen sits down next to him and receives a pint of something amber-colored with an almost cloyingly bitter odor. "Much appreciated," he says, and it is.

"Cheers," says Isaiah. "Haven't seen you around before, you new in town?"

"Sort of. Been here a couple months."

"Well, you found the right place." Isaiah sweeps his arm over Allen's view of the bar, as if presenting a prize on a game show. "Good thing, too. It's rough, getting settled in a new town."

Allen raises his glass. "Tell me about it."

"Yeah, that was me not too long ago. Well, twenty-two years ago. But who's counting?"

The bartender whistles. "You've been coming here since before I was allowed to cross the street by myself."

Isaiah shrugs. "Not *here* here, of course. This used to be a smoke shop, if I remember things right."

"Still, though."

"You been living here by yourself that whole time?" Allen asks.

Isaiah nods. "The whole time. Before that, too. I just prefer to be on my own, you know? Always have been, except for a brief stint living with my brother. My *actual* brother. Did not turn out well. He and I don't really talk."

"Sorry to hear it."

"Eh." Isaiah waves his hand. "Who needs family when you've got beer, am I right?" He and Allen clink glasses.

The conversation moves on from there, and mostly happens between Isaiah and the bartender. Allen chimes in every now and then, mostly to echo what one or the other of them is saying, but it's clear that he's no longer a necessary component of this interaction, which is fine. He prefers to let the older man go his own way, engross himself in sports and gossip, never asking about last names or brothers or absent families.

The similarities between the two of them are impossible to ignore, which, paradoxically, makes them far too easy to ignore for Allen. He expects this is the case for the other Allen as well. If their stories are really all that similar, then he probably understands how much it hurts, having to wrap your brain around impossible traumas all the time. He remembers everything—the morgue, the motel, the call center, what it was like to have half a body—but only in a sterile, theoretical sense of memory, the way he knows that the Earth is round without ever being able to see its roundness directly. He cannot hold the shape of it in his conscious mind. What's in there, in his past, is not something to be discussed with others, not because they wouldn't believe it, but because he doesn't think they could understand it. There is no support group for what he's been through, no online communities, no hashtags. There's really nothing to be done about any of it, except to live his life day by day, growing into something new. He may not be able to run from his past, but he can shift it into a part of his mind where it is more like a movie he saw years ago than something he personally experienced.

And so he has a few beers, reads a bit of his book, bids goodnight to the bartender and the man he is not related to as far as anyone knows, and takes the bus home.

Though drinking normally makes him tired, Allen finds that he can't sleep. He grumbles at nothing, rubs his eyes, but isn't disturbed. This is just the kind of thing that happens, living a life in which reality is not always on your side. He pushes himself out of bed, shuffles out to the kitchen, and sits at the table in front of the window where he left his pocket knife and the block of wood he's been whittling away at.

Allen tumbles the block around in his hand, a sawed-off piece of a two-by-four that he fished out of a roll-off dumpster by a construction site. He hasn't decided what it's going to be yet. A duck, maybe. He has sculpted three ducks already, over the past few months. He finds ducks relaxing, as a general concept: these soft, feathery little things that float around on ponds, looking for bread crumbs. A good choice when fighting insomnia.

I will start with the tail and work my way toward the head, he decides. He positions his hands on the table in front of him, block in the left, knife in the right. One hand to hold, one hand to carve. It's a satisfying sight: everything he needs, right here. Often, he finds it strange to think that he was ever less than enough for this.

EPILOGUE

IT'S A WONDERFUL night to have a brother, especially since it's also the shortest night of the year. Clove makes this joke every summer solstice. At this point, he is relatively sure that Ox at least gets the joke, though his brother's reaction never quite lets on whether he's amused or insulted. He keeps up the tradition mostly for the sake of consistency. Ox does, at the very least, appreciate when things are consistent.

In that vein, they enact most of the traditions. They grill impractically large cuts of meat, set off a firework or two, trace the movement of phantoms in the atmosphere as they stargaze. The one major difference, this year, is that Ox is the only guest.

This is because Clove has something to show him. Well, not Ox specifically, more like something to show his other friends and family who will, perhaps, appreciate it more. But he takes pride in his presentation, and when Clove shows his treasure to those people, he wants it to be good. Ox is more of a test audience. He's a man of narrow interests, and Clove means to temper his showmanship with the most frustratingly dismissive tools in the shed.

"It's nice having one solstice just to ourselves," says Ox, finishing a slice of coconut cream pie from the corner he's wedged himself in to rest his enormous, mossy antlers against the wall while he eats. "Much simpler. Cleaner. More like the way we hung out when we were young."

"We talkin' about the time you went after me with a band

saw on Halloween?" says Clove. Now that they've moved indoors, he's turned off all the lights to make Ox more comfortable, and can only see out of his wolf eye. He takes comfort in knowing that Ox has the kind of straightforward personality that doesn't necessitate constantly reading his tells during conversation.

"Among others," says Ox. "I miss the privacy of those days."

"Privacy," Clove repeats. "Now there's a real treasure. Still don't tend to get out much, myself. Can't get enough of that good, old-fashioned peace and quiet. You're not exactly the social butterfly yourself, if I remember."

"I play bridge," says Ox.

"Only the truly sick of mind play bridge." Clove collects their pie plates, buses them to the sink. "It's a psychopath's game, all built around the appearance of empathy masking the murderous instincts beneath. That's something I admire about you, Oxalis. You're never afraid to own what you are."

"Much the way I admire your tact, Clover." A flash of teeth appears below the great, luminous eyes in the corner, betraying that Ox is extremely proud of himself for this little bit of sarcasm.

"Tact is the purview of much younger men," says Clove. "When you get to be the age I am now—"

"I was the age you are now," says Ox. "Eight years ago."

"—you'll understand that all that tiptoeing around the truth to spare people's feelings is mainly just a symptom of a young man's impatience. Guys like me, on the other hand, who know we've got time to spare, prefer to either tell the truth straight up, or, more often, to cut it out of the picture entirely and bullshit full time. Life's much more entertaining that way."

"So you scorn tact *and* honesty," says Ox. "And you don't play bridge. Tell me, brother, just what is it that you *do* hold yourself accountable to?"

A wild grin spreads across Clove's face. He's heard it said

that his face is the most honest thing about him, and he supposes he'll just have to live with that. "Fun. That's the only thing *worth* being accountable to, Ox, and I hope one day you'll see that. On that note, how would you like to see the thing that I've cleared my schedule to show you?"

A tremor runs through Ox's skin, audible as a low, wet flapping sound, like a rug being beaten in the rain. A sheet of moss sloughs off one antler and splats on the floor. "I suppose."

Clove cracks his knuckles. "That's the spirit. Now, if you'll just follow me downstairs, we'll get the show started." He leads Ox through the kitchen and opens the hatch to the cellar.

"You expect me to climb down that flimsy ladder?" says Ox.

Clove kicks the leg of the ladder where it digs into the dirt floor. "More solid than it looks, I promise."

"I'll stay up here," says Ox. "There's no way I'd get through there without knocking my antlers on the ceiling."

"Aww, come on! You'll love it, I promise."

"I'll watch through the trap door," says Ox. "Whatever it is, you can show me from up here."

"Fine, but I'm giving myself some light, here. Can't see for shit." Clove doesn't wait for a response, but proceeds to the nearest kerosene lamp and lights it. Even though the lamp itself is well out of view of the cellar door, Ox winces as the radiant light hits his eyes. Clove crosses the room to the other trap door, the one set into the dirt floor, and flings it open. He reaches both arms into the darkness below, roots around until he feels a hand grip his wrist, and pulls up one half of a body, then the other. Hand-in-hand with each, he guides them into Ox's view at the bottom of the ladder.

Ox sees them, and snorts. "That's it? You picked up a couple nasnas to keep as pets? So what?"

"These aren't nasnas," says Clove. "They're humans."

"Ah," says one of the bodies through its half-formed mouth.

"Ah," the other one responds.

"Ah, ah." They go back and forth, echoing each other in tones that first rise in their volume and urgency, then begin to subside as the bodies grow tired of repeating themselves and satisfied that they've made themselves heard.

Ox nods. "Well, now you've got my attention."

"Glad to hear it, because this project has been almost a century in the making." Clove claps a hand onto each body's single shoulder, spins them both to face his brother. "Behold, the man who couldn't stand to be himself, and had to be his own brother too."

The first body—the one that forms the left side—looks at its equal and opposite side. "Ah. Ah! Ah, ah!" A tear starts to form in its eye.

"Ah?" says the right side. It reaches its hand out, apparently trying to touch the other body, but it misses and pokes Clove in the gut instead.

Ox runs a finger back and forth along his long jaw, from chin to throat. "How did you do it? They really seem to have lost all reason. It's extraordinary."

"Over and over, about once every three to five years," says Clove. "To answer your question. You know full well what I do with humans who decide they want to make a deal for a shortcut to their desires, but this finally answers the question: what happens to a human who wants something bad enough, desperately enough, that he truly doesn't care what it takes for him to get it, and is willing to suffer forever if he has to?"

"Show me the side where you cut them," says Ox.

"So glad you brought that up." Clove obliges, taking the right side in both hands and spinning it so his brother has a clear view of the thin, pink membrane that has grown in to hold the organs loosely in place. "Normally, they'd have grown a proper skin there by now, maybe even started to fill in where the rest of the body should be. The first few iterations had complete bodies by now. The later ones took longer, but this is the first pair for whom the growth seems to have stopped in its tracks at this stage."

Clove runs his hand gently over the right side's membrane and it winces from the pain, rewarding him with a few pained *Ah*s. "See what I mean, about suffering?"

"They really refuse to grow any further than this?" says Ox. "Fascinating. They truly don't mind being in such pain all the time?"

"Oh, they mind." Clove slaps the membrane with the back of his hand and the right side falls to the floor, shaking, soundless except for the occasional grunted monosyllable. Dirt clings to the membrane when it touches the floor. "Not minding something and being willing to put up with it are two very different propositions, as you can see. Turns out, you torture someone enough, and they come to see that pain as their only source of comfort, even as the constant discomfort wears on them. Remember, they *chose* this. They hurt themselves, over and over, *because* it comforts them. Because it's the only thing that's familiar."

"Can I have them?" says Ox.

"No, you greedy sonofabitch, you can't have them."

"Just one of them, then?" says Ox.

"I didn't do this for you," says Clove.

Ox pouts. "I thought you cared about fun. If I had one of these, that would be *very* fun."

The left side, still standing, turns its eye toward Ox and hops behind Clove. "Ah."

"Ah, ah," says the right side, unable to rise from the floor by itself. It reaches an arm toward Clove, but he doesn't offer help.

"Hold your horses, hold your horses," says Clove. "Come on, Ox, I've barely had a few months with these treasures. Let me play around with them for a year or two, then maybe I'll let you have one. Hell, maybe I'll let you have both, if you behave yourself."

"Hmm," says Ox. "I'm not always good at behaving myself, but I suppose I'll try, if I must."

"I appreciate that about you, Ox. Always trying."

"I hope I don't lose my patience again," says Ox, a slight warmth creeping into the tone of his voice. "If that happens, I might sneak into your cellar while you're not here. Might just take one without asking. And what a tragedy that would be."

"You even think about it," says Clove, "I'll put tapeworm eggs in your tea again."

"Ah, ah," says one of the bodies. Clove doesn't bother to look and see which one.

Instead, he begins ushering his treasures back toward the hatch he lifted them out of. "Well, I could sure go for a digestif. How about you? Got some good coffee and Irish Creme around."

Ox shakes his head, tossing moisture from his antlers onto the kitchen walls. "I'd go for a port wine, if you have it. I can't do coffee after dinner anymore. Keeps me up half the night if I'm lucky, all of it if I'm not."

"You don't say." Clove dusts off his hands on his trousers, having shut the door on the helpless twins. "Puts me right to sleep, if anything. How do you feel about mead?"

"Mead will do nicely." He offers Clove a hand up from the cellar, and Clove accepts.

"Why don't you head into the living room and make sure the fire's going nice and strong?" says Clove. "I'll pour us a couple glasses and bring 'em in."

"I'll watch you pour the drinks, if it's all the same to you," says Ox.

"That's my brother," Clove says jovially. He allows some little bit of satisfaction to creep into his voice, but only what seems conversationally appropriate. It wouldn't do to let Ox know how happy he truly is about his presentation of the brothers. That might give his elder brother ideas. You can't let Ox get ideas. He doesn't know what to do with them, and Clove has learned, over the centuries, that that's never as fun as he thinks it's going to be. Better to just let the man do whatever it is that he does with his time, and take up as little of Clove's as possible.

Down below, in a pitch black but strangely warm hole in the earth, two halves of a mouth utter monosyllables at each other and wait for him to return.

ABOUT THE AUTHOR

M.Shaw is a graduate of the Clarion Writers' Workshop (class of 2019) and an organizer of the Denver Mercury Poetry Slam. They live in Arvada, Colorado. Whatever you're reading, they probably wrote it in an empty art museum after midnight. They are on Twitter @shawwillsuffice.

ACKNOWLEDGEMENTS

Telling a story is one thing, but turning that story into a book requires the hearts and talents of a whole bunch of people. *One Hand to Hold, One Hand to Carve* would not be in your hands today without the diligence, enthusiasm and vision of Matt Blairstone and Alex Woodroe at Tenebrous Press, and of course the artistic contributions of Echo Echo. I doubt it would have gotten into Matt and Alex's hands without the help of Cooper Shrivastava, Eleni Linas, and Ann VanderMeer, all of whom read earlier versions of the manuscript and gave feedback that helped me mold it into its ideal shape. I'd never have met Cooper, Eleni or Ann if it weren't for the mentorship and community of the Clarion Science Fiction & Fantasy Writers' Workshop, which I attended in 2019. I attended Clarion on a Susan C. Petrey Scholarship, funded by Oregon Science Fiction Conventions, Inc. Every good book is a tree with deep roots.

I've also been very fortunate, over the course of my life, to be in a lot of rooms with a lot of amazing storytellers and great lovers of storytelling, whose encouragement shaped my own devotion to this art. I owe my thanks to my parents, Jerry and Sharon Tinianow; to Irina Bogomolova, Bennett Nieberg, Wheeler Light, Julie River, Hanif Abdurraqib, Julie Grawmeyer, Zach Hannah, Su Flatt, Betsy Clark, and the rest of my poetry community in Denver and Columbus; and to the rest of my Clarion cohort, Molly Bronstein, Elinam Agbo, Barton Aikman, Dan Stintzi, Forrest Love, Dianne Williams, Jamie Wahls, 'Pemi Aguda, Em North, Brady Nelson, Charlie Wrenwood, Yohanca Delgado, Jeremy Packert Burke, Alyssa Lomuscio, TJ Dimacali, Carmen Maria Machado, Karen Lord, Maurice Broaddus, Andy Duncan, Jeff VanderMeer, Shelley Streeby, and Patrick Coleman.

I'm sorry if I forgot anyone. You'll have to wait for the next book.

CONTENT WARNINGS

One Hand to Hold, One Hand to Carve
contains scenes that deal with:

*domestic psychological abuse

*abstract depictions of eating disorders

*allusions to self-harm/self-mutilation

Please be advised.

More information at
www.tenebrouspress.com

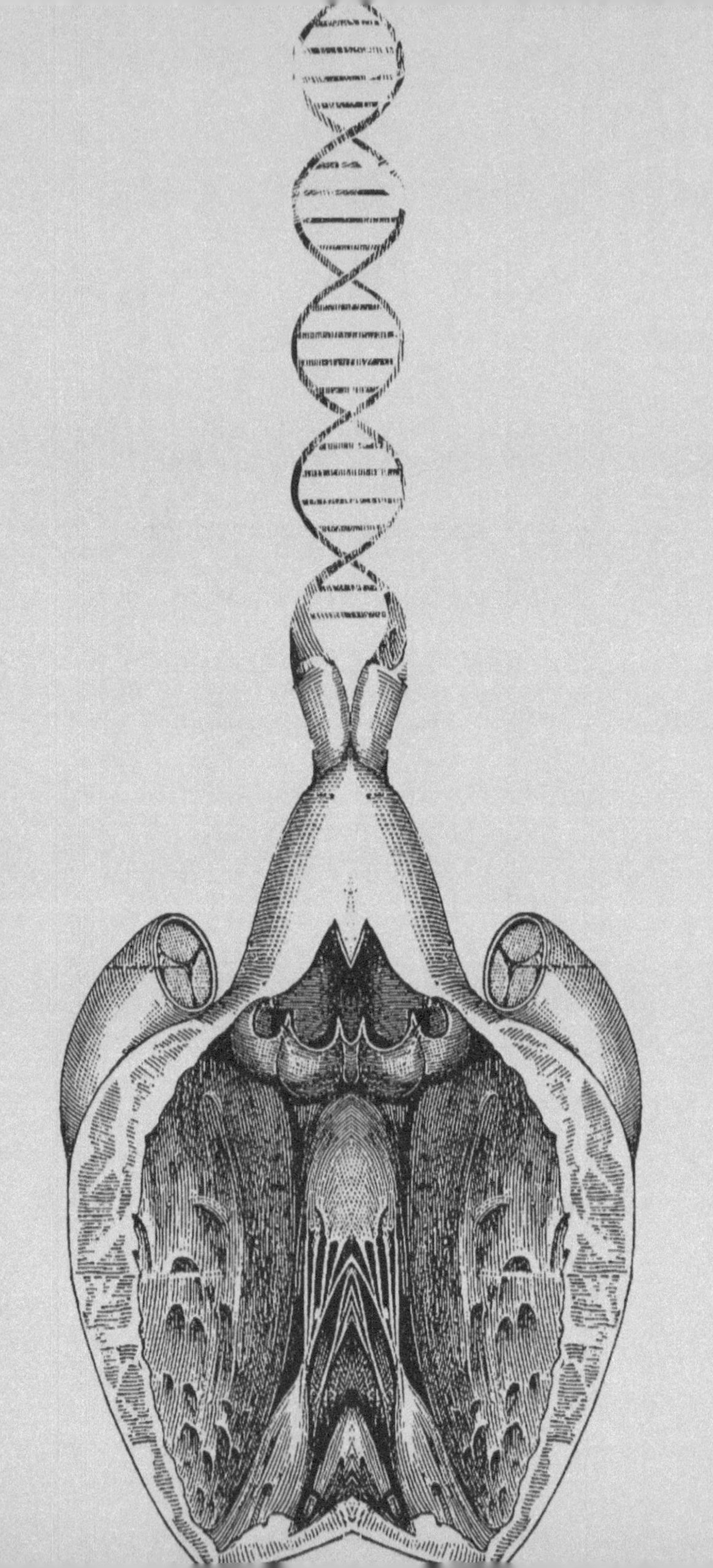

ABOUT TENEBROUS PRESS

Tenebrous Press was conceived in the Plague Year 2020 and unleashed, howling and feral, in spring 2021 to deliver the finest in transgressive, progressive Horror from diverse and unsung voices around the world.

We welcome the esoteric; the unorthodox; the finest in New Weird Horror.

FIND OUT MORE:
www.tenebrouspress.com
Twitter: @TenebrousPress

NEW WEIRD HORROR